The Enlightened Spaniel

A Dog's Quest to be a Buddhist

Gary Heads

Illustrations by Toby Ward

First published in Great Britain by Right Nuisance Publishing in 2019
This hardback edition published by Right Nuisance Publishing in 2021
Right Nuisance Publishing website address is
www.rightnuisancepublishing.com

Copyright © 2019 Gary Heads
Gary Heads has asserted his moral right under the Copyright, Designs and Patents Act, 1988, to be identified as the author of this work.
Illustrations by Toby Ward

All characters and events in this publication, other than those in the public domain, are fictitious and any resemblance to real persons, living or dead, is purely coincidental.

All rights reserved

This book is copyright material and must not be copied. reproduced, transferred, distributed, leased, licensed, or publicly performed or used in any way except as specifically permitted in writing by the publisher, as allowed under the terms and conditions under which it was purchased or as strictly permitted by applicable copyright law. Any unauthorized distribution or use of this text may be a direct infringement of the author's and publisher's rights, and those responsible may be liable in law accordingly.

ISBN hardback - 9781916446885

Also by Gary Heads

The Enlightened Spaniel – The Cat with One Life Left
The Enlightened Spaniel – The Stone of Truth

Animals have always been regarded in Buddhist thought as sentient beings. Furthermore, animals possess Buddha nature (according to the Mahāyāna school) and therefore potential for enlightenment. Moreover, the doctrine of rebirth held that any human could be reborn as animal, and any animal could be reborn as a human. An animal might be a reborn dead relative, and anybody who looked far enough back through his or her series of lives might come to believe every animal to be a distant relative. The Buddha expounded that sentient beings currently living in the animal realm have been our mothers, brothers, sisters, fathers, children and friends in past rebirths. One could not, therefore, make a hard distinction between moral rules applicable to animals and those applicable to humans; ultimately, humans and animals are part of a single family. They are all interconnected.

Even as a mother protects with her life
Her child, her only child
So, with a boundless heart
Should one cherish all living beings;
Radiating kindness over the entire world

for
Edna May

CONTENTS

The Beginning
1

The Present Moment
11

What the Buddha Said
30

Learning to sit all over again –Meditation
45

Silent Retreat
72

Reincarnation – I'm sure we have been here before
91

Karma – we have been good, honest
104

Loving Kindness – befriending next door's cat
126

Playing in the Field of Awareness
138

The Dharma, Dogma and The Ultimate Truth
154

The Monastery
166

The Transforming Power of Compassion
180

The World According to Half-Sister
193

1
The Beginning

"Mindfulness is a lifetime's journey along a path that ultimately leads nowhere, only to who you are."

Jon Kabat-Zinn

Far from being disheartened by the lack of reference to spaniels in the information gleaned from The Bookshelf's research, we find ourselves even more motivated to begin this journey.

IT ALL BEGAN ONE day with a simple observation fuelled by a spaniel's natural curiosity; that built-in inquisitiveness that all spaniels possess. On the other hand, it could just have been the instinct not to miss out on anything. In other words, nosiness. These curiosity-induced investigations have on occasions led to some startling results, like the discovery of food, or the homecoming of a long-lost tennis ball, or in worst-case scenarios, a trip to the vets.

First of all, the observation in question is not in itself an unusual one. Dad sneaking off to sit with his eyes closed like a statue in the upstairs office is, in fact, a regular occurrence in this house. We have heard him say on many occasions that he was going upstairs to do his meditation practice - in fact, we can't remember a time when he didn't do it. You could time him with your watch (if we had a watch that is). Armed with his meditation stool and blanket, he would disappear for thirty minutes on the dot, only re-emerging after the end of the meditation was announced by three chimes of a bell. During this period of meditation practice, nobody ever disturbed him. Not Mum, not Half-Sister, and certainly not me. Although he must have noticed a black nose under the door sniffing the air. The reason today is different from all the previous days we have witnessed this ritualistic event is basically down to our noses getting the better of us: we have overdosed on meddlesomeness. Therefore, we have decided that today is the day we will begin to find out what he is actually doing up in his office. We know he is meditating, but have no inkling as to what that's all about.

Concerted action is needed, and a thorough investigation into all things meditative is in order. Furthermore, we want to know why he is doing it in the first place (just in case we are missing out on something important).

Before I go any further, perhaps I should explain a few things first. For instance, you may have noticed I am using the pronoun 'we', and have referred to someone called Half-Sister. Rest assured these are connected. Half-Sister and I are springer spaniels, and are related by the fact that we both have the same Mum. As for our Dads, the least said about that the better. You can tell us apart due to my coat being black and white and Half-Sister's being liver and white. Although we are classed as working springers, we are yet to receive any recompense for our efforts. Another distinguishing feature that sets us apart is our build; we may be related but nobody in their right mind would suggest we could be twins. Just to clarify this point you might like to imagine Half-Sister and I competing at the Olympic games, (which upon reflection is more of a possibility than appearing at Crufts). You would find me lining up in the hundred metres sprint, whereas Half-Sister would be competing in the weightlifting. She would probably win.

I have to say that this quest to discover the secrets of meditation has been wholly instigated by yours truly. Half-Sister seems interested and eager to accompany me, but her motivation appears to be slightly different. I think it's more about the potential for extra snoozing or the chance of discovering more food that is driving her on. She is perhaps intent on broadening her belly rather than her mind.

Now, as you may have gathered we are no experts when it comes to the meditation business, but from what we can see it looks a lot like sleeping to us, and we are Zen masters at that. Like all good spaniels we will follow our noses and explore this phenomenon. After all, it may result in spaniels evolving to a higher level of consciousness, and if nothing else, that is an impressive sentence for a spaniel.

Now, as we pointed out earlier, Dad has practiced meditation for as long as we can remember. In fact, he teaches other people how to do it. He told Mum that they learn meditation to help them cope with stress and anxiety and to improve their overall wellbeing. Apparently with practice you can learn to respond to stressful situations in a more mindful and wise way, (this being the alternative to reacting and completely losing the plot).

We are thinking that this might be useful on those rare occasions that life's path deviates into slightly annoying occurrences. In those brief moments when your tail refuses to wag due to the Amazon delivery man not bringing the dog food on time, or all the tennis balls being under the settee and nobody shifting as they have been hypnotised by the television, or Half-Sister stealing the TV remote and moving into hostage-negotiator mode.

It feels to us like our curiosity and imagination have been captured by the subject of meditation. We are on the scent, sniffing for answers like two muddy spaniels in a field full of pheasants. If all these people are sitting still meditating then maybe it's time to drop the tennis ball, spit out the TV remote and see what it's all about. Well, for a little while anyway.

We don't have to look far to find clues about what meditation is or where it originated from. There are books on the subject everywhere in the house, especially by someone called the Buddha, often referred to as 'the Enlightened One'. It appears he recommended meditation practice and a lot of other stuff besides. There is even a book about non-doing. Now that's one for Half-Sister, as she does nothing all day and then carries on the next day because she wasn't finished.

Many of the books have very interesting titles and include words that are obviously part of the meditation dictionary. Words that appear often are 'way', 'path' and 'beyond', and it looks like you have to get on with it straight away too, because there are lots of references to 'now' and 'present moment'.

Whilst we were exploring all things meditative, (assisted by our good friend The Bookshelf), we stumbled upon a couple of really dusty books about how to train your springer spaniel. Good luck with that one. Obviously Mum and Dad thought it was a good idea at the time, before reality dropped in. Anyway, back to the path, way, beyond... whatever.

Upon reflection, we have come to the conclusion that you have to follow a path and that there should be no dawdling or sniffing along the way, as there is a certain degree of urgency. If you get lost then the Buddha is definitely the man to ask for directions.

However, after further investigation it turns out the path in question is not like a garden path, but more of a training path. This is tricky stuff and could take a great deal of effort on my part. The last time I ventured into training it took me three months to get into the swing of it, and that was just learning to wee outside. By all accounts, Half-Sister picked up house training in a flash, which is more than we can say about her self-control when play-biting as a puppy. Seems she was a bit of a wild child. She must have mellowed somewhat by the time I turned up and started hanging off her ears.

It seems that the breath plays a significant part in this meditation malarkey. We overheard a man talking about meditation on Dad's computer today, and he said that if it was down to us to remember to breathe, we would all be dead by now because we would forget. He also said that when we practise meditation we have to pay attention and concentrate on each breath, and when our mind wanders away, to gently bring it back and start again. He was doing well and being very informative, until he referred to 'returning the mind' as being a bit like training a puppy to sit. Perhaps he could give himself a treat every time he notices his mind wandering. What a cheek!

Who knows, if we get the hang of it, we might become enlightened ones like the Buddha. Now I know this would be an extraordinary achievement, but the thought of entering spaniel folklore is motivation enough to start this journey. An integral part of this adventure will be The Bookshelf. He hangs out in the dining room and is the fountain of knowledge in this household. If there is anything he doesn't know, it's not worth knowing. We are fortunate that Dad has brought home a multitude of books from his visits to the Buddhist monastery up the road, so the teachings of the Buddha abound. The Bookshelf is kindly making a study list, and has written down some very strange words, like *mindfulness*, *awareness*, *Dharma*, *Karma*, *reincarnation*, and *loving kindness* to name but a few. He also recited the following, written by someone called Jon Kabat-Zinn: "Mindfulness is a lifetime's journey along a path that ultimately leads nowhere, only to who you are." We think that is the most unhelpful sentence we have ever heard. If we went for walks on that path that leads nowhere, we would be ultimately lost and wouldn't know where we were, never mind who we are. It turns out that the person who said that is none other than the same person that referred to 'returning the mind' as being like training a puppy to sit. Say no more.

We are curious to discover if we are trailblazers on this spaniel meditation path, or whether there may have been brave and determined four-legged souls that have gone before us. The Bookshelf, who is always up for a bit of research, kindly offered to look into the matter and came up with the following facts, (his point of reference being meditation and dogs mentioned in the same book).

We are not sure if the Lhasa Apso practiced meditation, or even followed the Buddha's teachings for that matter, but this breed of dog certainly hung out with the right people, so had every opportunity. According to The Bookshelf, they were bred as interior sentinels in Buddhist monasteries in Tibet. Their job was to alert the monks to intruders. It's impressive that a dog could hold down such a responsible job, balancing the barking at intruders with the silence required when the monks were meditating. Although Half-Sister reckons it's no more impressive than retrieving pheasants without squishing them. She has a point.

The Bookshelf also uncovered a fascinating story about the Shih Tzu. This little dog originally came from Tibet and expanded its horizons to China. It must still have a sense of adventure, because the one we know lives down the street. Legend has it that the flash of white on its forehead is where the Buddha laid a finger in blessing, and that various parts of the Shih Tzu relate to Buddhism, all explained by the ancient symbolism attached to the breed. Now, we have no way of ascertaining whether the above is true or not; however it would be a great plus for us dogs if the ancient idea that the Shih Tzu has been blessed by the Buddha happened to be a fact!

After several hours of researching, The Bookshelf reluctantly informed us that he could find no reference to spaniels, meditation, or the Buddha in the same sentence. Being the gentle soul that he is he then proceeded to tell us all the fascinating facts and myths he did uncover about spaniels. For instance, it is said that William Wallace had a springer spaniel called Merlin, and that it even went into battle with him. Where was that in Braveheart? Then there was Millie, the springer who lived in the White House with President Bush Snr, and not forgetting Buster, who won the Dicken medal, (the animal equivalent of the Victoria Cross) for his bravery in the Iraq war.

As the collection of books on the subject is extensive, and The Bookshelf is always meticulous in his work, we have resigned ourselves to the fact that there is no mention of an enlightened spaniel, a meditating spaniel, or even a spaniel guardian of monasteries or temples to be found. Half-Sister rightly points out that we also have a white flash on our heads, and perhaps due to our renowned bum-wobbling and circle- spinning, the Buddha just couldn't get a handle on the blessing bit.

There is, however, a further option to consider (albeit a tad adventurous). This would involve getting ourselves to India or Nepal and joining in with the Hindu five-day- festival of Tihar. Dogs are worshipped at the festival by applying tika (the holy vermillion dot) on their forehead and draping them with garlands of marigold flowers. People that live in Nepal and India and follow the way of life referred to as Hinduism believe that dogs may guard the door of heaven, so you need to be nice to us dogs or you might not get in. We think more people need to know about this. Half-Sister has reflected on the Hindu festival of Tihar, and suggests that although garlands of flowers are a lovely gesture, they need to make sure they have lots of food. As for the dot on the forehead, that would be okay for a few days, as long as it washes off. It sounds like they know how to look after their dogs over there; however, as we don't have passports and would need the dreaded vaccinations, this is definitely a last resort.

Far from being disheartened by the lack of reference

to spaniels in the information gleaned from The Bookshelf's research, we find ourselves even more motivated to begin this journey. Half-Sister thinks we should be disciples of excellence and do our best to uphold the spaniel tradition. Therefore, after careful consideration, we are going to begin by following Dad's lead and learn how to meditate.

After our initial annoyance subsided regarding the Buddha giving the monastery job to the Lhasa Apso without us spaniels even being offered an interview (not to mention being passed over for the blessing), we eventually forgave him.

If our Dad has collected so many books about the teachings of the Buddha then he must think the Buddha is a wise man, and that his teachings are worth studying and putting into action. So, in addition to our meditation practice, we will also explore what the Buddha said, and see if we can incorporate some of that wisdom into our daily lives.

From today, our meditative journey to potential enlightenment begins. Half-Sister suggests we take time to reflect each day under the bamboo in the garden - it's her favourite spot. That sounds like a good idea to me. Who knows, in years to come, springer spaniels might research the subject and find us in the same sentence as *meditation* and *the Buddha*. Wish us luck - we might need it. Or, we might just be legends in the making.

2
The Present Moment

The present moment, if you think about it, is the only time there is. No matter what time it is, it is always now.

Marianne Williamson

According to Google, the present moment is the only thing where there is no time; it is the point between past and future.

BEFORE WE BEGIN THE serious business of learning to meditate, an essential part of our forthcoming journey to enlightenment, we thought we'd better check a few things out.

First stop: 'What is the present moment?' This is obviously important as it's mentioned at the beginning of nearly every book on meditation The Bookshelf possesses. In fact, in some books it is described as the only thing we have to work with. As our understanding of the present moment seems central to our learning, we have resorted to technology for a second opinion - this is by no means a criticism of The Bookshelf's abilities. According to Google, the present moment is the only thing where there is no time; it is the point between past and future. In other words, reality. By the way, it also states on Google that springer spaniels are even-tempered, gentle, friendly and sociable dogs that make great child companions; are **intelligent, skilful,** willing and obedient, and **quick-learners.** Please note the words in bold if you are thinking all this stuff is beyond the average spaniel, especially the intelligent and quick-learner bits.

Much to our surprise, we have discovered that human beings are prone to vacating the present moment on a regular basis. Apparently they spend a lot of their time either lost in the past or thinking about the future. When they are engaged in this mind-wandering, they can become distracted and therefore lose track of the present moment. This leads to an inability to fully concentrate on what they are doing.

Interesting. It's like when I am catching the ball in

the garden and suddenly a thought appears about dinner: in that moment I am distracted, and the ball hits me on the head. I have obviously moved out of the present moment into thinking about the future, thereby losing concentration. See, told you us springer spaniels are quick-learners! However, I don't lose concentration that often. Catching the ball is usually poetry in motion, unlike humans who are evidently always mind-wandering. We know this to be a fact because when we talk to them using spaniel telepathy, they just stare back all glassy-eyed and vacant-looking.

After putting our heads together, we have now come to the conclusion that this newfound knowledge could have significant benefits for Half-Sister and I, especially in the food department. If, as the theory suggests, Mum is constantly mind-wandering when she is preparing food in the kitchen, then the odds on her dropping stuff must be high, and it should only be a matter of patience and concentration. Half-Sister would be the first one to agree that she does not possess all the attributes on the Google spaniel list; however, when it comes to concentrating on food she is world-class. She even knows when the cheese is coming out the fridge before Mum knows she needs the cheese. Due to her expertise, Half-Sister has shared lots of invaluable tips with me over the years regarding food. These have included having a big drink after eating so you can get all the last bits out of the bowl, and always making sure you are positioned in the kitchen when the oven beeps. All this talk about food is making us hungry, so it might be a good idea to return to the present moment and the issue of mind-wandering.

To make matters worse, it appears human beings don't even know they are doing this mind-wandering stuff. They do it automatically. Seemingly this is why it is referred to as *automatic pilot*. They are certainly going down in our estimations - half the time there is nobody flying the plane!

Thinking back, I can recall a time when I was given Half-Sister's food by mistake. She gets different food to me because she has a habit of growing too much fat, but on this particular afternoon I got the stuff by mistake. At the time I thought nothing of it; a simple mistake. However, now that I have been educated in the ways of the human mind, I know exactly what caused it: automatic pilot.

In the opinion of us mere spaniels, it seems that human beings live in three parallel universes. Sometimes they spend their time wandering around the past, dredging up memories. At other times they can be found floating in the future, dreaming, planning, or worrying. Occasionally, (and it appears to us to be very occasionally), they visit the present moment, which is actually where it is all happening - or in the case of our dinner, not happening.

If they had only paid more attention, all would have been fine. The appropriate dinner would have been dished out and everyone would have been happy, although Half-Sister was very happy to get my dinner instead of hers. Incidentally, after a bit of research, it turns out that the man talking on the computer is none other than Jon Kabat-Zinn. He is judged to be a bit of an expert when it comes to the *automatic pilot* business and suggests the opposite is something called 'mindfulness'. He explained very nicely that "mindfulness is paying attention, in a particular way, on purpose, in the present moment, and non-judgementally." We have taken that on board, but prefer the spaniel version: *watch* what you're doing, right now, especially in the food department, but I'll let you off, this time! As he is an expert in the field and we have lots of his books, we have decided to follow his advice. Just to show there are no hard feelings, we are not judging his puppy-reference anymore, and may even venture down *the path to nowhere* one day.

Eating Meditation

We have discovered today that when human beings learn mindfulness, they start with an eating meditation in the very first week. This practice not only highlights the issue of automatic pilot, but also aids the skill of noticing things, an important aspect of staying in the present moment.

Food choices that humans favour in this particular practice include raisins, grapes, or chocolate (blimey, all toxic for dogs - we could be dead before we have a chance to notice anything, and at the very least we could be practicing our observational skills from the vets waiting room!) After careful consideration with Half-Sister, who is suddenly right into mindfulness practice by the way, we have decided to partake in a carrot meditation, and as we eat them every day a bit of automatic pilot might be creeping in.

We have borrowed a book on mindfulness from The Bookshelf, and sure enough one of the first exercises it recommends is the eating meditation. Even better, the first chapter includes a transcript of the practice. The instructions carefully explain that we have to explore the carrot with something called *beginner's mind*, which means we have to look at it as if we have never seen it before. We will definitely need to focus our beginner's mind, as the fridge is currently *full* of carrots, not to mention how many there are in the supermarket. This could be a challenge. Following the instructions to the letter, we start by noticing the shape. Conclusion: it's carrot-shaped. Then we explore the colour. Orange with dirty bits. Systematically, bit-by-bit, we pay careful attention and explore what this carrot looks like, how it feels, if it has a smell, and even how heavy it is in the paw.

I have to admit that I am finding this exercise *very* interesting. I never knew how much there was to a carrot! Most of the time when I am eating one, I have to concentrate on crunching it as fast as possible in case Half-Sister pays a visit to hoover up. Talking of Half-Sister, her carrot meditation seems to have taken a turn for the worse. The guidance from the book seems to have gone completely out the window as she is currently repeating to herself over and over: "It's a carrot', it's a carrot, it's a carrot." Unperturbed by her chattering teeth and circle-dancing, I crack on regardless.

It's now time to see if the carrot makes any kind of noise when we hold it up to our ears. I have to report that the result of this is total silence, although Half-

Sister does point out that if we bite it there *will* be a sound. I ignore that statement and continue as per the instructions.

Now, everybody knows how sensitive a springer spaniel's nose is, so if this carrot has any kind of smell, we will detect it. Holding the carrot to the nose, we check for odour; after a thorough inspection, we are rather disappointed to report that it simply smells orangey. The next section of the exercise is slightly worrying, so to clarify we have it right we have decided to read the instructions twice. 'Put the object (carrot) in the mouth and just leave it there, noticing any sensations that are arising in the body.' At this point, Half-Sister is just shaking her head and is on her fourth carrot already. The sensible option would be to continue this journey of exploration single-pawed and leave her to it.

With the carroty object firmly placed in the mouth, I begin to tune in to any sensations that might be arising. Well, the overriding sensation that has arisen in this moment is the need to wee, as concentration on all this mindfulness-business has led to me forgetting to notice that sensation. I'm sure it goes against the theory, but the wee will have to wait a while, so it's back to the eating meditation.

Shifting my mind firmly back into exploration mode, the first thing I notice is just how heavy the carrot feels in the mouth. This is quickly followed by an overwhelming urge to eat it. I am also sensing that things are getting a bit salivary, and all teeth seem primed for action. With the tummy rumbling like Mum's washing machine on maximum, I decide that is long enough, and it's time to move on to the eating bit.

After consulting the instructions once again, it suggests that I now take just one bite and then explore what arises, so putting my best teeth forward I do just that. Half-Sister looks impressed with the effort; however, she has lost track of how many carrots she has eaten and there seems to be an orange tint about her. The crunch from biting the carrot is epic; it fills my whole head and sends a ripple down the body, all the way to the tip of the tail. Finally, I am allowed to chew it very slowly and then swallow it when I'm ready. I have to admit that the aforementioned carrot was possibly the best one I have ever eaten; this paying attention stuff is cool! I noticed so many sensations that I wouldn't normally be aware of that a conversation with Half-Sister, the resident food-guru, is in order. However, before I have time to discuss the eating meditation practice, one overriding sensation returns with a vengeance: I gotta go.

We've been looking at the world as if it is a giant carrot.

We have been thinking, well, pondering really (us spaniels like a good ponder). The result of all this reflection is that if we have been missing all this stuff about a carrot, it would be logical to assume that we might have been missing loads of other things in our day-to-day excursions. To test out this theory, we are venturing into the back garden as if we have never been there before.

My family have lived in this house for fourteen years. As I am four, it's the only place I can remember. Half-Sister can go back another two years as she is six. You would think after all this time we would know what the back garden looked like; however, after our experience with the eating meditation, we are beginning to wonder if that's actually true.

Before we begin the garden meditation, we have taken time to consult our old pal The Bookshelf to see if there is anything else we should take with us apart from *beginner's mind*. Much to our surprise, there appears to be a whole raft of mindfulness attitudes we will need to take into the garden besides *beginner's mind*. There is *non-judging*, *patience*, *trust*, *non-striving*, *acceptance*, and *letting go*. Blimey, we will need the wheelbarrow for that little lot! Half-Sister has kindly offered to carry *non-striving*.

Upon stepping into the garden, the first thing we notice is that the ants are out in force. They are funny little things - they always look to us as if they can't quite make up their mind as to what direction they should go in and are getting stressed by the responsibility of making a decision. Half-Sister and I study them for a while and decide that the mindfulness attitude best-suited to this situation is acceptance; after all it's their garden too. If they give the impression that they are very busy but are actually only going in circles, then who are we to judge? We are not averse to a bit of circle-spinning ourselves. I am about to move on when half a dozen of the little blighters start running through my toes, and half-way up my legs. Consulting the list of mindfulness attitudes is extremely tricky, due to the excess tickling sensations and listening to Half-Sister's instructions to just eat them. In the end we decide on *non-striving* and just let them do their thing. They soon get bored and are drawn back to their circle-dancing - seems we also used *letting go* without even realising it.

For the next hour or so we mindfully pay attention to whatever we notice in the back garden. We explore the grass, soil, plants, trees, flowers, and all the little creatures, bees, wasps and butterflies. Some things appear to be hardly moving, whilst others come and go in the blink of an eye. However, the thing that has captured our interest the most are the birds. When you get a good look at them they do look rather strange. It is as if they have just dropped in from another planet. We are now curious to discover where they actually do come from. Half-Sister's explanation that they come from the sky is not, in the cold light of day, incorrect, but on this occasion, we will go with the expertise of The Bookshelf, who has kindly explained the following:

The present scientific consensus is that birds are a group of theropod dinosaurs that originated during the Mesozoic Era

Yes, you heard that right, there are indeed dinosaurs flying around the garden, and this *amazing* fact would have lain buried but for beginner's mind and a bit of research by The Bookshelf. It seems that developing present moment attention is well worth the effort, as is working with the mindfulness attitudes, which definitely warrants further investigation.

As the mindfulness attitudes are difficult for a beginner to grasp, especially a springer spaniel beginner, we have decided to sit in the sunshine under the bamboo and carefully read the explanation for each one. Hopefully this will allow us to understand their meanings, and therefore how we begin to incorporate them into our daily lives. The bamboo is our favourite spot in the garden, and is perfect for reflection and peace and quiet (apart from the odd visit from a flying dinosaur).

Beginner's mind

The richness of present moment experience is the richness of life itself. Too often we let our thinking and our beliefs about what we 'know' prevent us from seeing things as they really are. We tend to take ordinary for granted and fail to grasp the extra-ordinariness of the ordinary. To see the richness of the present moment, we need to cultivate what has been called 'beginner's mind,' a mind that is willing to see everything as if for the first time.

After studying the above explanation and gazing at each other with beginner's mind, we have come to the following conclusion: if we wander into the back garden and don't pay attention then we are in danger of just thinking about the garden, rather than experiencing what it is like to actually be in the garden. As we have visited the garden thousands of times before, we could miss what it looks like in this moment because we have shifted into automatic pilot. If we pay attention, we will see the garden and everything in it as it actually is right now, in the present moment, as if we are arriving in the garden for the very first time. Half-Sister, who is suffering from a carrot-induced headache, tells me that having studied me with her beginner's mind, she has come to the conclusion that I am extraordinarily ordinary.

Non-Judging

Mindfulness is cultivated by assuming the stance of an impartial witness to your own experience. To do this requires that you become aware of the constant stream of judging and reacting to inner and outer experiences that we are all normally caught up in and learn to step back from it. When we begin practising paying attention to the activity of our own mind, it is common to discover and be surprised by the fact that we are constantly generating judgments about our experience.

After reading the above, Half-Sister has volunteered to be the 'impartial witness', and has gone off to sit in the constant stream of judging and reacting. This seems to involve sitting under the big bamboo in the back garden thinking (or snoozing - it's hard to tell). This has apparently done nothing for her carrot-induced headache, and so the explanation of the above is down to yours truly.

As far as I can see, the attitude of non-judging is encouraging us to be present with the actual experience, instead of thinking that we are going to like it or not like it, or remembering the last time, or projecting how we think it's all going to turn out. The best example I can think of is going for a walk. I like walking, but if it happens to be pouring with rain, my mind tells me it's going to be nasty, soggy and smelly. Yet, when we get out in the rain, it's great! I get lovely and muddy and have a fun fight with Dad when he tries to restore me to my original colour. It seems to me that thoughts are one thing, and reality is another thing altogether.

Patience

Patience is a form of wisdom. It demonstrates that we understand and accept the fact that sometimes things must unfold in their own time. A child might try to help a butterfly to emerge by breaking open its chrysalis. Usually the butterfly doesn't benefit from this. Any adult knows that the butterfly can only emerge in its own time; that the process cannot be hurried.

Half-Sister and I like butterflies. They always seem happy in their work. We like to watch them and chase them; we don't know if that's wisdom or just fun, or perhaps it's both? As for patience, well, we have oodles of that! I can sit in the garden all day on the off-chance that someone will emerge from the house and throw a ball. Usually it's only a matter of time. If, however, I get bored and try to force the issue with high-pitched barking, I usually end up being banished to the house. It seems that it is wise to stay patient, silent and focused. Half-Sister, meanwhile, can patiently wait for a treat until the sun goes down (carrots excluded).

Trust

Developing a basic trust in yourself and your feelings is an integral part of meditation training. It is far better to trust in your intuition and your own authority, even if you make some mistakes along the way, than to always look outside of yourself for guidance. If at any time something does not feel right to you, why not honour your feelings?

Many people seem to be of the opinion that dogs are simply guided by their noses, or in Half-Sister's case her belly. What many fail to appreciate is that a spaniel's intuition is a thing to behold. When this intuition is added to the aforementioned nose guidance system we get head hunted for all the top jobs. We are employed to rescue people off mountains, sniff out drugs at the airport, or get recruited into the army to find roadside bombs. This intuitive skill was no more evident than the time we visited Grandad's house and Half-Sister sniffed out a Malteser from under his fridge. He had no idea it was there, or recollection of even buying them in the first place. In terms of honouring our feelings, that is easy - if it feels right to us, we wag our tails. If it doesn't, we bark. If people look sad, it's time for a cuddle.

Non-Striving

Almost everything we do is for a purpose - to get something or somewhere. But in meditation this attitude can be a real obstacle. That is because meditation is different from all other human activities. Although it takes a lot of work and energy of a certain kind, ultimately meditation is non-doing. It has no goal except for you to be yourself. The irony is that you already are.

After reading the above explanation, I think I am in danger of catching Half-Sister's headache. Due to the complexity of the subject, it might be wise to take this bit-by-bit. The statement regarding *non-striving* seems to be suggesting that everything we do is for a purpose, or to get something or somewhere. We agreed with that bit. The fact that meditation is different from all other human activities might be helpful to humans, but is not so helpful if you happen to be a spaniel. It appears that meditating takes a lot of work and energy, but is basically doing nothing. Half-Sister opens one eye from under the bamboo and confirms that, in her opinion, this is indeed true. So there is no goal other than to just to be ourselves. That's easy - we are always ourselves.

Acceptance

Acceptance means seeing things as they actually are in the present. If you have a headache, accept that you have a headache. If you are overweight, why not accept it as a description of your body at this time? Sooner or later we have to come to terms with things as they are and accept them. Often acceptance is only reached after we have gone through very emotion-filled periods of denial and then anger. These stages are a natural progression in the process of coming to terms with what is.

The person who wrote that explanation of acceptance must be clairvoyant, or telepathic, or both. Who do we know that fits that bill? We need look no further than under the bamboo. Uncanny. Accepting things as they are in the present moment. I am black and white, Half-Sister is liver and white, but we accept that we are both springer spaniels. It is as it is.

Letting Go

They say in India there is a particularly clever way of catching monkeys. As the story goes, hunters cut a hole in a coconut that is just big enough for a monkey to put its hand through. Then they drill two smaller holes in the other end, pass a wire through and secure the coconut to the base of a tree. Then they put a banana inside of the coconut and hide. The monkey comes down, puts its hand in and takes hold of the banana. The hole is crafted so that the open hand can go in but the fist cannot get out. All the monkey has to do is let go of the banana. But it seems most monkeys do not let go. Often our minds get us caught in very much the same way, in spite of our intelligence. For this reason, cultivating the attitude of letting go, or non-attachment, is fundamental to the practice of mindfulness. When we start paying attention to our inner experience, we rapidly discover that there are certain thoughts, feelings and situations that our mind seems to want to hold on to.

We like that explanation; it makes sense. Unless you're a monkey. We have no idea how the banana feels about it. The place to begin the practice of *letting go*, or *non-attachment,* would seem to be with my obsession with tennis balls. I can get very attached to them, and rarely let them go. For others who shall remain nameless but can be currently found under the bamboo, the TV remote is a no-brainer.

After carefully scrutinizing the mindfulness attitudes, we have unanimously decided that developing the skill of mindfulness through the regular practice of meditation would be a wise move. We are going to need to instil a bit of discipline to maintain our daily practice, and also accept that the journey might be a *tad* challenging at times. However, the good news is that mindfulness is not something we have to acquire, but rather something we have to remember. We were very mindful as puppies, but have let things slip. We might have been born with the skill and practised paying attention at puppy-training classes, but now we can get a bit bogged down with remembering the past and projecting into the future. Being more mindful will help us explore what is actually happening in the present moment, rather than what we think might be happening. The mindfulness attitudes appear to be of great importance, and the general consensus seems to be that they will form the building blocks of our practice. Half-Sister reminds me that building blocks can fall down with the wag of a tail; however you can keep rebuilding them until the foundations are solid, or you can simply be more mindful of your tail.

Upon reflection under the bamboo

We have come to the conclusion that cultivating the mindfulness attitudes will take a great deal of practice, especially as we are not only trying to bring them into the meditations, but also our day-to-day life. It would perhaps be a good start if we actually learnt to meditate. This is our next step and, with practice, we can hopefully begin to be more mindful spaniels. According to The Bookshelf, a good way to remember to be mindful is to choose something that can act as a bell of mindfulness. When you see or hear your chosen sound or object, it helps to remind you to bring your attention back to the present moment. I have decided that there is no better object suited to the task of being a bell of mindfulness than Half-Sister. She can be my mindfulness reminder, albeit a big one. Every time I see her, I shall refer to the mindfulness attitudes. I will look at her with beginner's mind, as if she has just arrived for the first time. There will be no judging, endless patience, no striving to change anything, trust in those spaniel instincts, and acceptance of things as they are. Last-but-not-least, I shall let go of the banana. As for the present moment, it seems we need to accept that the man on the computer was right all along. It appears that this is all there is, so we'd better learn how to pay attention to it, otherwise we will miss everything. Before we embark on our first meditation practice, we think it would be wise to refer to head office and see what the Buddha actually said about all this stuff. This will require a visit to consult with our old mate The Bookshelf, the keeper of all knowledge in our house. He has books called 'What the Buddha Said,' and 'In the Buddha's Words' to name just two; however, judging by the thickness of them, the Buddha had an awful lot to say on the subject. Added to this, there are all the books about meditation practice and the Buddha's teachings given free by the Buddhist monastery. There is lots to contemplate, oodles to learn, and hours of practice ahead. Maybe one day we will even visit the Buddhist monastery (that's if we can get past that pesky Lhasa Apso on the door).

3
What the Buddha Said

Do not dwell in the past, do not dream of the future, concentrate the mind on the present moment. Three things cannot be long hidden: the sun, the moon, and the truth. All that we are is the result of what we have thought.
Buddha

It looks to us like the long walk through the woods is comparable to our journey through life; with the right understanding and intention, that journey will be a richer experience.

WHEN IT COMES TO seeking information, The Bookshelf can usually be relied upon to come up with the goods; however, when we asked him to explain to us the teachings of the Buddha, his answer was most unhelpful. He informed us that if we were to take every book he possessed on the subject and study it intently, we may eventually acquire an inkling of the essence of the Buddha's teachings. We can only assume that he is slightly overwhelmed by the volume of text, or he simply got out of the box on the wrong side. Half-Sister thinks he is not quite right this morning and is acting as if he is one volume short of an encyclopaedia. We have decided that diplomacy is the best course of action, and so have let go of any bookshelf input for the moment. On a more positive note, we are happy to report that the following statement was found in a book about the Buddha, chosen at random. We have to say that it has filled us with inspiration and motivation to begin our quest.

Buddhism affirms the unity of all living beings. All equally possess the Buddha-nature, and all have the potential to become Buddhas, that is, to become fully and perfectly enlightened. Among the sentient, there are no second-class citizens. According to Buddhist teaching, human beings do not have a privileged, special place above and beyond that of the rest of life. The world is not a creation specifically for the benefit and pleasure of human beings. Furthermore, in some circumstances in accordance with their Karma, humans can be reborn as humans and **animals can be reborn as humans***.*

Yes, you did read that correctly. Animals can be reborn as humans, and that obviously includes springer spaniels. After reading that sentence several times we are afraid to report that we got a little carried away with this and let our imagination run riot with regard to what or who we would like to come back as. Upon reflection, we would not be averse to returning as springer spaniels, providing we had the same standard of owners, the same sized garden, and remained a double-act. If we were fortunate enough to get an upgrade to human beings (although the word upgrade is somewhat debatable), I might plump for a tennis star with an endless supply of tennis balls. I could be famous for chewing all the yellow off the balls during the breaks. Half-Sister has pondered long and hard on this subject and is seriously considering coming back either as a psychiatrist, or a TV repairman. Make of that what you will. Of course, this depends on whether you actually have a choice in the matter - it might just be potluck, or all down to *Karma* (whatever that is).

There is so much information regarding what the Buddha actually said, coupled with the fact that he said it thousands of years ago, that we find ourselves in a bit of a dilemma as to where to begin. It states in our book about the Buddha that originally his teachings were passed down and memorised by his followers. Now that's a lot to remember, and we all know that stories that are passed down have a habit of being prone to exaggeration (my escapades on holiday a few years back being a prime example). The farmer who owned the farmhouse where we were staying reckoned I would be fine in the garden, as the wall was too high for me to jump. After I legged it and rounded up all the chickens he retracted that statement. Over the years, as the story has been passed down, the wall has gotten higher and higher and the chickens are now accompanied by ducks and turkeys. If I were able to jump the new version of the wall, I would be on Sky News. Fortunately, as the Buddha was a thoughtful man, he has kindly left us some practical guidelines and practices to follow, and as any springer spaniel owner will know, we are always up for a bit of training and learning new things.

It is interesting that the Buddha, apart from being a prince, was actually just an ordinary man who through his own efforts developed an understanding of the universe. He then very kindly decided to share his teachings with those that were interested, hence the arrival of Buddhism and Buddhists, although The Bookshelf is quick to point out that Buddhism it is *not* a religion, but rather a philosophy. Half-Sister in the meantime has been occupying herself by researching where springer spaniels come from, and has unearthed some interesting facts. She has found a reference as far back as 17AD, and apparently we come from Spain (Hispania). It seems we arrived in Britain with the Romans. Half-Sister also informs me that we originally came from a reputable springer spaniel breeder in the Lake District, and that most recently she came from the kitchen. Reading about the Buddha's life has got us wondering. We know he had a wife and a son, but the big question is this – did he have a dog, and if so what kind was it? As he was a prince, he could have presumably afforded a pedigree, rather than a heinzy beanzy fifty-seven variety bit-of-this, bit-of-that version. Of course, his choice would have be determined by which dog breeders were in the vicinity, or which mutts were hanging out in the local rescue centre. We think a springer spaniel would have been top of his list due to our intelligence, willingness to learn and our aptitude for mixing with royalty. As both Princess Grace of Monaco, and Princess Mary of Denmark had springer spaniels, maybe the Buddha started the trend? It must have been a difficult choice when he upped sticks and left his family behind in search of enlightenment, but the burning question is: did he take his dog with him? Unfortunately, we will probably never find the answer to that question, so for now we will just have to imagine the Buddha setting off on his quest with his springer spaniel in tow, its ears gently flapping in the wind and its nose pressed to the ground. Half-Sister tells me that the last sentence is called *artistic licence*.

All things considered, it appears to us that after the Buddha reached enlightenment he did his best to help other people reach enlightenment too. We are fortunate to have the method he used detailed in his teachings, and if we dedicate the time to following the guidelines and practices there is every chance we will also find the ultimate state of reality and peace. Half-Sister thinks that this ultimate state of reality and peace may well lie under the settee alongside the dusty tennis balls and tumbleweed, but is happy to be proven wrong.

As far as we can ascertain, if you're a Buddhist, you believe that life is a cycle of birth, death and rebirth. In spaniel-language that's hello, goodbye, and I'm back again. However, you have to be very careful with your actions, not only right now, but also in the past, because this affects what you come back as in your next life and how your life is going to play out. In other words, everything from a three-legged blind cat with half a tail to a human being who owns a dog food business is up for grabs. This is the power of what the Buddha calls *Karma*, so if you approach every action with this in mind, you will naturally form an internal moral standard by which to live.

The first thing we have discovered is that the Buddha put a lot of emphasis on teaching something called *The Four Noble Truths*. He did this in order to show people the true nature of reality. By following and thereby understanding these truths, you can follow a path that leads all the way to enlightenment. In fact 2,500 years ago he stated, "I teach suffering, its origin, cessation and path, and that's all I teach." Half-Sister thinks that's a bit of an understatement - a bit like saying I won Cruft's but all I did was walk around in a circle. It appears to be true, however, that *The Four Noble Truths* contain the essence of the Buddha's teachings, and that he came to understand these four principles during his meditation under a bodhi tree in Bodh Gaya in India. That sounds a bit like our reflections under the bamboo in the garden. Seems Half-Sister's idea is indeed a good one.

We think that you could almost compare the Buddha

to a vet, albeit without the injections and the other stuff (we will not mention what goes on when you are facing in the wrong direction). The reason we are making this comparison is that in the first Noble Truth, the Buddha diagnosed the problem - suffering - then in the second Noble Truth he identified the cause. In the third Noble Truth he realised there was a cure. Then in the fourth Noble Truth he sets out the Eightfold Path, which is the prescription, a way to end suffering. Half-Sister has been considering all this and has likened it to the local woods where there are four paths; they are signposted yellow, green, blue, and red. Unlike the Buddha's paths the paths in the woods seem to work in reverse order. The yellow path is easy-peezy - a stroll in the woods. Green is easy, but due to the hills, makes your tongue hang out. Blue takes ages and you need to keep stopping for a rest, and red goes on forever - you get lost and need a lie down (suffering).

Anyway, continuing on, what is *The Noble Eightfold Path*? What's it all about, and how do we follow it? From the information gleaned from Dad's books and the Internet, the first thing we have discovered is that everything on the path appears to begin with 'right'. This has confused Half-Sister, who suggests that if we continually go right on the path we will meet ourselves coming back. Maybe she is on to something and that's how it works, although she doesn't look convinced. One thing that has got the Half-Sister seal of approval is the Buddha insisting that his teaching is not a dogma, and is to be questioned, rather than accepted as the truth. Although she doesn't quite understand what that's all about, it's still nice to get a mention. As it's a sunny day outside, we have decided that our best option is to take everything we have collected so far under the bamboo and indulge in some right pondering.

The first step on the Eightfold Path appears to be **Right Understanding,** although some books refer to it as **Right View.** Regardless of which one you use, it is obviously an important first step on the path as it relates to seeing the world and everything in it as it is, rather than as we believe it, or want it to be. After going around in circles for a while, which is always helpful, we have concluded that this is like going for a walk in strange woods. On our walks, we always stop to check out the notice board. There is usually a map, directions, and a guide to how long it should take you compiled by a man with extremely long legs. This man must cover a large area, as all our walks take much longer that the suggested time. Studying all the information is important before you set out on a journey but it is only preparation - it's not the journey itself. After taking in all the information, you could now be worrying that it will be too hard, or take too long, or be comparing it to other walks. However, it's only the experience of undertaking the journey that will lead us to see things as they actually are - in other words, *Right Understanding*. After all that pondering, we have decided to have a little snooze before tackling step two.

Upon waking some time later, Half-Sister informs me that she was dreaming that she was the Buddha's dog, and that her name was Right Nuisance. That's interesting, as I have heard many people call her that over the years.

The second step on the Eightfold Path is **Right Intent**; this is the step that sets our intention and commitment to see the journey through with passion and persistence. *Right Intent* involves seeing that all life is equal, thereby bringing compassion to it all. It is important to include yourself when bringing compassion to life; in fact it is probably the place to start. From the corner of my eye I can see that Half-Sister has a large frown plastered on her face. This is down to her wondering if when the Buddha wrote that all life is equal, he was aware of cats. If he was then there is much work to do. Obviously the Buddha's dog, Right Nuisance, had no input here. Going back to our long walk in the strange woods theory, it seems to us that we need to know the terrain and be aware of any potential problems that might arise. We need to have the right gear for the trip and be aware of everyone else that's coming along. This is similar to *Right Understanding*; however, we will only make it to the end if we have the passion for the journey - the right intention. It looks to us like the long walk through the woods is comparable to our journey through life; with the right understanding and intention, that journey will be a richer experience.

Step three. **Right Speech** (friendly and inappropriate barking). The Buddha informs us that we tend to underestimate the power of speech, and often regret things we have said in haste. We have all experienced the disappointment that arises when we get told off, whether justified or not, and also the good feeling we get when we are praised. This happens to us every time we charge around the garden in the pouring rain and mud. It's a great game, and it is what springer spaniels are renowned for. When we skid into the kitchen to show we have been proudly upholding the spaniel tradition, we just get told off for the state we are in, and for the redecorating job we have done on the floor. In the very next moment we get praised for standing still while we are getting cleaned up! Talk about confusing human behaviour. That being said, we can also think of other incidences when we fall into this state of chaotic and reactive communication. As I mentioned earlier, my downfall is barking in the back garden because nobody will come out and throw the ball. They usually do play with me, but not if I bark. I think it's now become a habit. A very counterproductive one. In Half-Sister's case it's barking for her dinner. Even though it's been prepared, in her opinion it's not being done fast enough. The more she barks, the longer she is made to wait. However, both those examples pale into insignificance when compared to our play-fighting in the living room when they are trying to watch the telly. They have to pause the programme because they can't hear for all the growling and rolling on the floor (that's if they have the TV remote in the first place - it is not unusual for Half-Sister to play fight and steal the remote all in one movement). Maybe one day they will understand that this game is all about getting their attention and encouraging them to join in. The TV is bad for them, unless it's David Attenborough, football or tennis. To summarise (as we seem to have digressed a little) *Right Speech* is about speaking the truth and having an awareness of the impact of one's harsh speech. Half-Sister suggests that if you can't say anything nice, it is best to say nothing at all. Although she is happy to follow her own advice, she seems less inclined to take on board that *Right Speech* would also include idle barking and spreading rumours about next door's cat.

The encouragement to take an ethical approach to life, considering others and our world, is the essence of **Right Action**, the fourth step on the path. It would also include keeping to agreements and not taking what has not been given. Half-Sister's tendency to pinch dog biscuits out of the post lady's pocket when she is not looking would *definitely* fall into this category. *Right Action* also incorporates the *Five Precepts* that were given by the Buddha. They are: not to kill, steal, lie, indulge in sexual misconduct, or take drugs or other intoxicants. If we use the TV as reference, human beings appear to have their work cut out when it comes to adopting an ethical approach to life. They would do well to listen to the Buddha. The next bit is our favourite, and we encourage everyone to take heed. *Right Action* includes a whole approach to the environment and, wherever possible, the *Right Action* should be taken to safeguard the world for future generations, including puppies.

If the work you do or how you spend your day does

not respect all life, then the progress you make on *The Noble Eightfold Path* will be limited. Therefore, to address this, the Buddha introduced the fifth step: **Right Livelihood**. As the Buddha said, all living beings are equal, so how you spend your days should reflect that equality. Certain types of work were not recommended by the Buddha, especially dealing in drugs, intoxicants or weapons. *Right Livelihood* also implies that some kind of community work is beneficial; we recommend the springer spaniel rescue centre if you are feeling brave, although that might be a step-too-far for some.

Now, the sixth step could have been designed specifically for springer spaniels. It's called **Right Effort**, and means cultivating enthusiasm and a positive attitude in a balanced way. Making sure that you are not too tense or impatient, not too slack or laid-back, but rather cultivating an attitude of steady and cheerful determination, both in meditation practice and in bringing the Buddha's teachings into daily life. Bearing all of that in mind, if you then put (springer spaniel) in the Google search engine, this is what you will find:

> *Springer spaniels are happy, smiling dogs with a great zest for life. They are steady, cheerful and determined.*

Bingo. The Buddha could well have been talking about springer spaniels. Half-Sister thinks the odds on Right Nuisance being the Buddha's dog have just been slashed. The Bookshelf has told us that today bookstores are full of books about positive thinking, so the Buddha was well-ahead of his time with his thoughts on the power of having the right attitude. *Right Effort*, positive thinking, followed by focused action.

Okay, six down, two to go. Whilst the last one seemed easy enough to get to grips with, the next step is a little bit tricky. This is because it involves changing the way you think about stuff. It's called **Right Mindfulness** and means being aware of the moment and being fully present in that moment. It reminds me of when we are travelling in the car - we spent our time listening to sounds, seeing the trees passing by, tuning into the movement and thinking. This usually includes thoughts about where we are going, when we will we get there, and when we might be coming back. Sometimes all this happens before we have even moved off the drive at our house or in some cases, before we have actually gotten into the car. Our understanding of *Right Mindfulness* is that instead of all this mind-wandering, we should endeavour to be aware of the journey in each moment, to do our best to be clear and undistracted rather than being lost in past or future thoughts. By being aware, we can notice old patterns of thinking, habits and the fears we sometimes have about the future, or regrets about the past. Half-Sister thinks that being mindful sounds a lot like when you are completely absorbed in what you are doing and your mind is only with that one activity. Like eating your tea, or chewing your foot, or in my case, pulling the yellow strands off the tennis ball, one-by-one. The Buddha seems to be showing us how we can bring that kind of awareness into daily life.

Eventually we arrive at the very last step on *The Noble Eightfold Path*, which is **Right Concentration.** *Right Concentration* helps us to focus on an object in meditation practice. Our attention could be on the breath, the body, sounds, thoughts, emotions or feelings. Alternatively we could focus on a flower, a lit candle, or even the concept of kindness. The last two elements of *The Noble Eightfold Path* are important in as much as they help us see things as they actually are, not as we think they might be. Developing *Right Mindfulness* and *Right Concentration* opens the door to reality.

Upon reflection under the bamboo

As we suspected, the Buddha had an awful lot to say, all of it very wise but perhaps a bit too much for a springer spaniel to fully comprehend, unless of course we keep practising through a multitude of lives as per the reincarnation theory. For now, having studied *The Four Noble Truths* and *The Noble Eightfold Path*, we have decided that we will endeavour to do our best with that little lot. Any queries or subjects that need further research will be referred to The Bookshelf, who is basking in his new-found responsibility. Half-Sister is encouraged by the fact that she may be a direct descendant of the Buddha's dog, Right Nuisance, and therefore have a head start on the path to enlightenment. Only time will tell. All this studying of the Buddha's teachings has led us to believe that if everyone followed his advice, the planet would perhaps be a better place, and everybody might be a lot happier. We are inspired by the words of Mahatma Gandhi who we discovered in our book rummage: "Be the change that you wish to see in the world." In honour of Right Nuisance, we are going to give it our best shot. Right. How do you meditate?

4
Learning to sit all over again – Meditation

If you have time to breathe you have time to meditate. You breathe when you walk. You breathe when you stand. You breathe when you lie down.

Ajahn Amaro

Half-Sister, on the other hand, has chosen to adopt an undignified posture in the corner of the office

Mindfulness of breathing

HAVING DONE THE NECESSARY research and uncovered some CDs belonging to Dad we are now ready to begin developing our meditation practice. As he has gone to work today, we have taken the opportunity to sneak into his office; apart from it being the quietest place in the house, we also thought all the previous meditation energy might do us good. However, it appears I am flying solo on this trip as Half-Sister has informed me that she is here simply for moral support and to give me the occasional paw if I fall asleep. Now, at puppy class we remember not only being taught to sit, but also learning how to pay attention. It would seem that these skills are also necessary in meditation. It looks like I might have a head start on my meditative journey, although paying attention was never my forte. That was always Half-Sister's domain.

The first instruction to weave its way into my floppy ears is to adopt a dignified posture, and as the CDs are designed for human beings, I have taken the liberty of amending the guidelines to suit springer spaniels (or any other dog for that matter). To begin the task of creating a dignified posture, I have to first place the paws firmly on the floor. This seemingly gives a sense of being grounded and transports me into the present moment. The guidance continues at a gentle pace, and I am informed that it is best to have the back straight, but not rigid-at ease. To comply with the (at ease) bit, I have decided to switch the nose into neutral and let the ears hang loosely either side of the face. Splendid.

Half-Sister, on the other hand, has chosen to adopt an undignified posture in the corner of the office. This involves all four paws being in the air, her belly (and everything else for that matter) pointing at the ceiling and one leg twitching. If that wasn't bad enough, she completes the picture with some *very* loud snoring and the occasional sigh. So much for keeping an eye on any potential snoozyness from yours truly. As the saying goes, you can choose your pals but you can't choose your relatives.

It's now time to gently close my eyes and bring awareness to sensations in the body, beginning with any that I notice from having my paws placed firmly on the ground. After exploring my paws for a while I am then instructed to tune into any sensations arising from what I am sitting on. I have to say that this sounds a bit weird to me, and slightly dangerous. The fact that Half-Sister has chosen to sit out this meditation might be a blessing in disguise. However, as I am a mere novice in the meditation business it is not my place to argue, so as instructed I pay attention to all the sensations emanating from what I am sitting on - my bum. It is recommended that I take a little time with this 'grounding' bit, as it's an important part of the experience, so I do just that. It's all very interesting; not only can I feel the contact with my fur and paws on the floor, but there is also an awareness of the air and the space all around me. After a while I find myself nicely settled in and chilled. Unfortunately this state of spaniel bliss is shattered by the next instruction, which is to take the attention to the belly and feel the breath rise on an in-breath and fall on an out-breath. Half-Sister, hearing the words belly and sensations in the same sentence, has arisen from her undignified posture on the off-chance we could be launching into another eating meditation. Upon realising that it is only the breath that is the focus of attention, she simply gives a big sigh and flips back into her undignified snoring posture. I am encouraged to take a little time to 'surf' these breaths, riding with them as they flow like waves on the ocean. It's all very rhythmic, and the desire to join Half-Sister in an undignified posture is calling. I remember having watched dogs surfing on the television. Half-Sister has suggested I rephrase that statement to avoid confusion; not dogs surfing on top of the telly, but rather surfing the waves on the sea in a programme on the TV. Anyway, the movement reminded me of travelling in the car, which is not a good thing given my chequered history of travel sickness, so we won't go there. Perhaps it would be better to just stay with the in and out, shake it all about bit. Half-Sister concurs before resuming her impersonation of unconsciousness. The voice on the CD trundles on enthusiastically - it's time to explore other parts of the body that move with the breath. This includes the mouth, nose, throat, chest, and even the tail. After exploring the movement of the body and breath for a while, I am then instructed to move on to the place in the body where the sensations of the breath are most prominent. Well, that's definitely the end my nose so, focusing my attention, I follow each in-breath and out-breath from the shiny black place. Fascinating. The recording encourages me to bring curiosity to this process, or 'spaniel inquisitiveness' as it's known in the trade, noticing the gaps in between breaths, and how long and deep the breaths are. This is all intriguing stuff, and makes you appreciate what a fine job the breath does. Everything seems to be progressing nicely; however, there is something that has been bothering me during this practice. The frequency that my wandering-mind has been legging it off to pastures new. According to the authority on the CD, this is apparently okay. It's just what minds do. When it happens, I am just to notice it and come back to following the breath. I am reassured by the next statement telling me that it's the nature of the mind to wander. Half-Sister, who has suddenly dipped back into consciousness, chirps up that her mind has wandered to the kitchen to see if dinner is ready and has yet to return. Well, at least she has noticed. After ten minutes that felt like a fortnight, it's time to bring the breathing meditation to an end. To complete the practice, I have to expand my attention to the whole of my body and then to an awareness of being in the room. That's it - job done. After the meditation is completed, Half-Sister leaves the room with the following statement: "We should not rule out the possibility that the hokey-kokey is actually what it's all about." Enough said.

Nose to tail meditation – body scan

Having survived the first meditation practice, we are now confidently moving on to tackle the next CD. Humans call this practice the *'body scan meditation'*. It seems to involve taking your attention around the body and noticing any sensations as you go, and as we discovered in the previous meditation, you also have to keep an eye out for Wandering Mind. The body scan is normally done lying on the floor in a position that appears remarkably similar to Half-Sister's undignified posture. Contrary to my initial thoughts that Half-Sister might be a natural for the body scan, she has instead decided to sit this one out. This is all due to the fact that it is a variation of a traditional Burmese practice called '*sweeping*', and in the book it suggests it's a bit like a CAT scan. That suggestion was all that was needed to end any thoughts of Half-Sister's participation. It looks like I am on the lonesome trail again.

The meditation begins with an invitation to close your eyes before gathering your attention and exploring how it feels to be now lying on the floor. Well, tuning into arising sensations including those from Dad's meditation cushion and blanket found under his desk, I immediately notice that my recently acquired undignified posture feels comfy, cosy and sleepy. Unfortunately, at this point in the meditation I have to report that Wandering Mind is off on one already. It took her a milli-second before she began thinking that comfy, cosy and sleepy could be the meditation dwarfs from the film Snow White. Better start again before the 'Hi Ho' song makes an appearance. Right, how does it feel to be lying on the floor again? The voice on the CD implies that you can't do the meditation practice wrong, and apparently you can't do it right either; there is no right way, and no wrong way. The idea is to bring awareness to sensations in the body just as they are in the moment. This means not trying to create a certain state, like snoozing, or relaxing. I am also encouraged to do my best to accept that sometimes there will be periods when there will be no sensations at all. Zilch. This is also fine - it's just our experience in the moment. I'd better just pause here for a moment to get this right in my mind. So, there is no right way or wrong way, and no special state to be created. If there are no sensations, I'm not dead - it's just my experience in the moment. Sound.

Now that I am nicely settled in my undignified posture and have clarified that whatever experience arises is worthy of an A*, I am happy to move on to the next part of the body scan practice. Following the guided instructions on the CD, I now shift my attention to the breath. The guidance suggests that it is helpful to find the place where I can feel the breath the most and then to tune in to all the sensations being created in the body from this point. After scouting around the body for a while, I finally decide to stick with the end of my nose, as per my previous meditation excursion. Off we go. In-breath, out-breath, in-breath, out-breath. Now at some point during the proceedings the 'Hi Ho' song from Snow White arrives with a vengeance. The harder I try to get rid of it the louder it gets, and just to expatiate the situation, more people keep arriving to join in and sing along. In-breath, out-breath, in-breath, out-breath... After bringing the mind back a zillion times I finally settle into the rhythm of my breath entering and leaving the body.

The breath is described in this meditation CD as '*an anchor to the present moment*'. Like a ship floating in the harbour, the anchor holds it in place when it wanders away, so our attention is returned to the breath when we notice it has been taken away by the tides of distraction. Now that makes a lot of sense to me because my ship has been all around the globe, into outer space and back again, and it's not me that's been steering it, but rather that mutineering little pirate Wandering Mind.

Eventually, with a little help from first-mate-Awareness, I am able to wrestle control of the ship back from Wandering Mind and I'm ready to set sail on a journey around the body. As per the guidance, I park the breath in the background for a while before taking my attention all the way down the legs and out to the tips of my toes. It is recommended that I take Curiosity and Beginner's Mind with me on this trip and do my best to just let arising sensations simply come and go like ships in the night. I'm not supposed to move my toes and create sensations, but rather just pay attention to what is happening, or not happening, right now in the present moment. The lady on the recording, who sounds very nice, suggests that I might notice tingling, numbness, heat or coolness, but has said nothing about furriness, which is my overriding sensation. Now she is telling me to explore each individual toe, including all the spaces in between. Eventually, after sufficient time has elapsed to appease the teacher on the CD, it's time to pay attention to the bottom of my feet, and then the top of my feet. After what seems like a lifetime, she finally moves on to my legs, which have been patiently waiting but are now bordering on fidgety eagerness. It comes as no surprise when the inevitable statement arrives: 'The mind will naturally wander away from the practice.' What a revelation. Not. Again, she tells me that this is not a mistake and that I should just acknowledge where it has been and return my attention to the body scan meditation. However, I am going to have a word with Wandering Mind before I continue the practice. It might be natural for the mind to wander, but it's also natural for me to be annoyed with the little devil. So I ask her very nicely where she has been when we are supposed to be paying attention. She rather sheepishly replies that spending so much time exploring the toes, coupled with that woman's monotonous voice, was doing her head in. She just had to get away. Sometime later she found herself wandering aimlessly in the past before, much to her surprise, realising that she had somehow stumbled into the future. All this was beginning to freak her out until she fortunately bumped into Awareness, who explained that she was busy practicing the body scan and perhaps she would like to follow her. Blimey, it's like trying to herd cats! By the time we all get back to the meditation, the teacher has moved on to the body. At this stage of the body scan I would just like to point out that as the CD I am using is made for human beings, there are some bits that she is on about that I don't have. As I am having to improvise and adapt as I go along, I have decided that the best course of action is to begin at the end of the tail and work upwards. Unfortunately, it seems that Wandering Mind gets bored with any part of the body, and Awareness is going to be exhausted by the time we reach the head (if we ever reach the head that is). Anyone who has ever had a springer spaniel will tell you that we don't just wag our tails; it's more like a full body wag at speed, so paying attention to the tail being still is hard-going. Upon reflection, the tail may not have been the best place to start, as I have discovered that anticipation can run through the whole body, making it difficult to concentrate. Fortunately, the middle part of the body was a bit easier to explore with rumbling belly sensations, fast-beating-heart, twitching, and warm bits all discovered and held in awareness. My meditative observations are only interrupted by the presence of Wandering Mind staggering through parallel universes, totally oblivious to what is real and what is not.

Eventually I arrive at my head after a brief detour to explore the neck. By this time, Curiosity is on her knees and has completely lost interest in the proceedings, whilst Beginner's Mind is adamant she has been here before. That lady on the recording suggests I bring back Wandering Mind gently but firmly. That's fine for her to say but you have to find the little blighter first! Unperturbed by all these distractions, I continue on with the meditation, taking time to investigate any sensations that are arising in the area of the throat, jaw, mouth and my lovely spaniel ears. Next, it's time to notice any sensations in and around my nose. It's wet, sniffy, airy and twitchy. I am now instructed to gather my attention and explore the eyes. As I have them closed, it's sensations of darkness that arise. That was easy! Finally, I reach the very top of my head. The final instruction is to take the breath and guide it through the whole body, as if the whole body is breathing. Just as I complete the final part of the meditation, Wandering Mind skids in, and for the first time today enquires with a sentence that has an element of curiosity: "What did I miss?" She is swiftly followed by Awareness, who suggests we might like to consider tying the anchor mentioned on the CD to Wandering Mind's feet. Alerted by the sound of the three bells that signify the end of the practice, Half-Sister arrives to check for any taints of cat. After a quick tour of Dad's office, she proclaims that the coast is clear.

Paws and breath – walking meditation

The mind can go in a thousand directions, but on this beautiful path, I walk in peace. With each step, the wind blows a flower blooms.

Thich Nhat Hanh

The '*Walking meditation*' is supposedly one of the simplest and most accessible forms of meditation to practice, (well, according to the instructions on the CD cover that is). However, as I am discovering, this is nearly *always* followed up with the statement, 'simple, but not easy'. This time, the meditation is all about paying attention to the experience of walking. Not just going for a walk and spending half the time thinking, but rather *knowing* that you are walking by tuning into all the sensations in the bottom of your feet. Why is walking meditation not easy, you might ask, and why would we not know we were going for a walk? Of course, it's that pesky Wandering Mind again. That little gal is starting to annoy me big-time. Evidently, when we practice walking meditation there isn't a goal, or even a destination. We just arrive in each moment. It suggests on the CD that when I have cracked this mindful walking business, it could transform my walks in daily life. I shall look forward to that one, although my walks are good fun anyway. Let's be honest here - when I am out walking or playing in the garden, it's my nose that leads the way, not the paws. They just follow my nose. Another thing to consider is, unlike humans, I have *four* paws to pay attention to. That means twice the effort! I have been thinking about there being no goal or destination in the walking meditation. Although I understand the principles behind it, I can't help but think that this is a skill that could give me an edge in a certain situation. When I stalk next door's ginger tom cat, I move very slowly and mindfully, so although it states that there is no goal, perhaps, through practising the walking meditation, I can also develop my sneaking mindfully skills. This might allow me to get close enough to scare the little blighter, as he currently seems to have eyes in the back of his head. If all else fails, I can always resort to Half-Sister's technique of digging a hole under next-door's fence. This has led to some spectacular results over the years, although the ginger one next door might disagree with that one.

Before I begin the practice of walking meditation, I

first have to find a place where I will be relatively undisturbed, somewhere that is comparatively quiet and with enough space to walk backwards and forwards on my journey to nowhere. I have chosen the living room, as it is quiet and has a very colourful soft rug that is just the right length to walk on. An invitation has gone out to Half-Sister to join me on this trek to no place in particular, but she informs me she is otherwise engaged in practicing her undignified posture and chewing her foot. She also informs me that if the walking practice has no destination, I could be in for a long trek and to be sure not to miss dinner.

Prior to taking my first step, I thought I'd better explain that there is a bit of a dilemma with regard to the walking meditation. This is due to the recording I have found, having been recorded by none other than my Dad. The issue in question is not in itself a problem - I can handle it - but it will be the first time I have ever followed his instructions word for word. How weird is that? Anyway it's time to start. The first instruction issued by my Dad is to come to stand. As I'm already standing that takes care of that. I am to let the breath flow freely, and it appears we are starting with a short body scan - as I am quite short this should be *perfect*. Once again, it's time to explore any sensations created by the paws being in contact with the floor. Feeling the support of the ground beneath, maybe a sense of being rooted and grounded, and bringing awareness to the whole body, standing. The next instruction according to Dad is to gently shift all the weight down the left side and into the left leg, and then to notice any sensations this movement has created.

What sensations can I notice? Well, there is wobbliness for a start, and a bit of lop-sidedness. After a while, it's back to standing straight and then shifting all the weight down the right side into the right leg. Tuning in, I notice right-wobbliness, and right lop-sidedness. Simple. We are now moving on to lifting the foot, or in my case the paw, so we come back to centre and slowly raise the right paw. Now here is my predicament. I can adapt the human instruction to raising the right paw, which I do all the time anyway - it's in-bred as we are hunting dogs and it means we are ready for action. Reflecting for a moment on the built-in retrieving ability that follows the raising of either paw, I lift the right (Half-Sister the left by the way). I think we naturally retrieve things very mindfully anyway. For instance, when I bring back tennis balls its always done right in the moment and with total focus. Half-Sister also has this skill, but rarely wastes energy lifting a paw or retrieving a tennis ball. She has been known to lift the occasional paw for effect, usually for a photo opportunity or the possibility of a treat. Saying that, I do remember her catching a crow once on a walk and then not letting Mum have it; Mum eventually had to phone a friend for assistance. They had to hold her nose until she spat it out (Half-Sister's nose that is not Mum's). After all the commotion it just flew away totally unharmed and unsquished. Half-Sister had held it very mindfully.

I'm afraid I got a bit distracted and wandered into the past there. She's a tricky little customer is Wandering Mind. Anyway, lifting my paw and retrieving the mind, I am back. Where were we? Oh yes, adapting. I can raise the right paw; however, this means the back-right paw misses out. I could try lifting them both, but fear I might be launching into spaniel yoga and an overriding sensation of falling-overness. In the end I decide to alternate and give everybody a go.

Following Dad's guidance, I raise the front-right paw and place it just in front of me, as he suggests all that is needed is an incy-wincy, little step. I then raise the back-right paw, followed by the front-left paw, and then the back-left paw, all the time tuning in to all the sensations that are being created as I walk. I am just getting the hang of the walking meditation when guess who arrives to put me off my stride? Who else but Wandering Mind. She immediately launches into a torrent of questions and I forget where I am in the practice. "Are ya being a robot?" "What's the point of this game?" "Have ya forgotten how to walk?" "Let's do something else", "I'm bored!" No sooner does she arrive than she's gone again. Silence returns, and the sensations in my paws are once again being noticed. However, just like scooting next-door's cat, sooner or later she will be back to pester me again. Lifting, moving, placing, the rhythm of paws on the ground continues as they make their merry way to the land of nothingness, until eventually Wandering Mind returns with yet another question. "If you don't have a goal or a destination, how will you know when you get there?" Fortunately I don't need to find the answer to that one as the bells on the recording ring to signify the end. Taking a moment to reflect on the walking meditation, I have come to the conclusion that I rather like it. It makes me appreciate just how long it took to learn to walk when I was a puppy, and how I now take it for granted. Automatic pilot. It also seemed to calm down Wandering Mind, who returned less and less as the practice progressed.

Sit, leave, and pay attention – sitting meditation

You should sit in meditation for twenty minutes a day, unless you are busy, then you should sit for an hour.

Old Zen saying

According to The Bookshelf, the *sitting meditation* has been practiced in one form or another for thousands of years; therefore this ancient practice is obviously a *very* important element of our training pathway. He has advised us that we will need to be focused and concentrated if we are to understand and develop the skills required to engage with this practice. Rather than being daunted by his statement, we are looking at things in a positive manner and reflecting upon all the weeks we spent at puppy training classes, endlessly paying attention and concentrating on commands. Although we only went for the treats, it seems all that hard work could be about to pay off in the *'sitting meditation'*. Half-Sister excelled in her class - she could sit and wait patiently for commands forever. It could get dark and she *still* wouldn't budge an inch. All she needed was the motivation of food. Me, I can take it or leave it. Give me a tennis ball though and that's a completely different story. I can even retrieve the ball when it's pitch black in the garden, or catch it in my mouth in mid-air (that one always impresses Dad). Unfortunately none of the above skills were needed in puppy training classes, so I fell well short of Half-Sister's standards. Speaking of Half-Sister, I am pleased to report that unlike previous meditations, she has decided to join me. This is due to the importance placed on this practice by The Bookshelf, and the fact that there are no references to cats in this one.

Having done our due diligence before embarking on the sitting meditation, we can confirm that The Bookshelf appears to be correct in his assumption that the practice is a key element on the path to enlightenment. We also discovered that difficult and unpleasant moments are just part of the flow of daily life, just like the pleasant moments. This is in keeping with the Buddha's proclamation that suffering is a natural part of life. Half-Sister reckons that if Awareness is tuned into arising thoughts, emotions, feelings and sensations, she can help us be more mindful and respond in a more skilful way. She can be the bouncer at the nightclub of Phenomena.

Continuing our pre-meditation research, it appears that in general we react to experiences in one of the following ways:

Indifference (not bothered)

This is when the content of the present moment is deemed to be irrelevant, boring or uninteresting. So,

Wandering Mind decides it's not worth hanging about and goes off to find something she thinks is more interesting, and then gets lost in thought. What a surprise!

Attachment (tennis ball syndrome)

This is explained as wanting to hold on to experiences that are happening in the moment, or wanting an experience that is not happening in the moment. This is a biggy for us spaniels, especially where tennis balls and treats are concerned. Half-Sister is attached to cuddles, so when it's not happening, she steals things for attention or bats you with her paw. Well that's my psychological viewpoint anyway. As for my tennis ball attachment, that's a lost cause or a visit to the dog whisperer (although I always have trouble hearing what he is on about).

Aversion (take it away, or let's not go there)

As far as we can ascertain, aversion seems to be about the need to get rid of an experience or trying to avoid one that's coming down the road. Classic examples that come to mind are a car journey, or a trip to the vets, or a double-whammy of a car journey to the vets. In Half-Sister's case, it's going in the bath. Everyone in the house has an aversion to that one. All of the above examples can cause us problems; however a regular meditation practice can help us learn to respond to them more mindfully. Even Half-Sister's Titanic impression might be included in this category, albeit with a lot of practice.

Now that our research is complete, it's time to adopt our dignified postures once again and begin the sitting meditation. As per previous instructions, we have to find a place with not too many distractions or interruptions, where we can still the body and unwag the tail, so it's back to Dad's office we go. The voice on the CD then announces that we are going to move from '*doing mode*' to '*non-doing mode*' and just be in the moment. We are instructed to do our best to bring patience and kindness to our unfolding experiences moment-by-moment. Half-Sister informs me that she awoke in non-doing mode, so has been primed for action since breakfast.

Breathing

Somewhere in between, breathing out and breathing in.

Kate Bush

After settling into our dignified postures, we begin the meditation by noticing the fact that we are breathing. It's always good to know you are still breathing, otherwise the whole meditation will be non-doing with intense stillness and an overall sensation of being dead. I am happy to confirm that Half-Sister and I are definitely breathing. We can feel our breath and can see our ears going up and down - always a good sign. We have to do our best to follow the in-breath from the beginning to the very end, and then follow the out-breath from the beginning to the very end. Repeat as required. Again, we have to focus our attention on the part of the body where we can sense the breath the most. Due to the success of our last effort, we have stuck with our noses as the preferred choice. After several breaths, we are once again reminded by the meditation teacher on the recording that sooner or later Wandering Mind will arrive unannounced and eager to take us someplace else, anywhere else. Inevitable. As she thinks the breath is boring and doesn't deserve this much attention, she continually skedaddles off. Time is of the essence as far as Wandering Mind is concerned, with so many things to revisit, make up or analyse, she has to move fast to fit it all in. The trouble is every time she distracts us, Awareness has to go off and collect her and we have to start all over again. Eventually we are back with the breath and being encouraged by the guidance to let go of any thoughts around trying to control the breath. Instead, we are endeavouring to let it just breathe itself - in other words, it breathes all day so it's the expert. Who are we to interfere? As we get up close to the breath, we notice the spaces in between breaths. This is where the breath has a little rest, taking a breather from all that in-out activity. You might think that all breaths are the same, but they are not. Well, ours aren't anyway. Some breaths are short, some are long. There are slow breaths, fast breaths, smooth ones, rough ones and splutterly ones, just like when I drink the water in my bowl too fast. On we go, exploring our breaths and bringing friendly Curiosity to our breathing, whilst bringing our attention back over and over again as Wandering Mind repeatedly does her thing. Even though she is a constant pain, we are beginning to become quite fond of her (in a naughty child kind of way).

The Body

Take care of your body. It's the only place you have to live.

Jim Rohn

It's now time to expand our awareness to include a sense of the body and any sensations that happen to be floating about. We decide that a good place to start is noticing any sensations arising from having our paws and bums on the floor. After a while, we then open our awareness further to include the touch of our collars and the overall furriness of our bodies. As per the instructions, we do our best not to judge the sensations but accept them as our experience in the moment. The guidance then moves on to sensations that arise in the body that are intense and difficult to stay with. We are given a variety of options should the need arise, like moving, breathing into them, or taking our attention to the breath. However, Half-Sister suggests that as we are not in tents, just in Dad's office, we can miss that bit out. Following a period of exploring experiences in the body, including hot bits, cool bits, wet bits and itchy bits to name just a few, we are now ready to move on to the next section of the meditation.

Sound

> *The temple bell stops but I still hear the sound coming out of the flowers.*
>
> Matsuo Basho

It's time to expand our awareness yet again. This time we are paying attention to the arising and passing of sounds. Worryingly, it suggests on the CD that this could be a sound arising from within the body. I have therefore taken the precaution of stepping away from Half-Sister. The other possibilities of a sound from inside or outside the room appear less troublesome. Curiosity is the name of the game here, and we are encouraged to notice if the sounds are near, far away, constant or coming and going. Apparently we don't need to search for the sounds either, but rather just let them come to us. That all sounds feasible, but the next instruction to do our best not to judge the sounds might be tricky. Just listening to sounds without liking or disliking, or even labelling them, is difficult enough, but as we are about to discover, there is an extra hindrance around the corner. Now, why this is extra-difficult to do is not hard to work out. No sooner had we begun than Wandering Mind decides to join in because, unlike everything else we had engaged in so far, this bit seems like fun. Every time we listen intently to a sound, doing our best not to label or judge it, we are greeted by the meditation equivalent of a football fan shouting at the referee. This interplay of annoyance goes something like this: we listen, Wandering Mind tells us what she thinks it is. Tweet, tweet - Dickey birds! Chime-chime - ice cream man! Whirly-whirly - Helicopter! And so it goes, on and on and on. Even as we move to the next phase of the meditation she is still at it.

Thinking

> *Very little is needed to make a happy life; it is all within yourself, in your way of thinking.*
> Marcus Aurelius

Before our wandering-mind-induced headaches reaches new levels of intensity we are saved by the guidance moving to the next section. This may, however, be a very short reprieve as we are expanding our awareness to thinking - noticing our thoughts as they scuttle through the mind. It is recommended that we perhaps view our thoughts as simply mental events that arise and pass - a bit like how we listened to sounds really - coming and going. These arising and passing thoughts could be about anything; they could be memories, thoughts about food, the garden, the vets, going for walks - all pretty random really. If we happen to meet Wandering Mind, which we surely will, we will endeavour to come back to watching our thoughts as soon as we can. How long that takes is anyone's guess, as we are visitors in her hometown and she knows the terrain inside-out. The recording reassures us that it's fine to observe thoughts in whatever way we can. One example is to imagine sitting in the garden, watching clouds come and go. Clouds, like thoughts, move at different speeds: fast, slow, meandering. Some don't even look as if they are moving at all, but they are. This idea appeals, so we settle in the garden under the bamboo in our mind for a bit of cloud-watching. Who knows - we might even spot the red kite that floats above our house. For some, thoughts might surface as words, be spoken or appear as pictures or videos; however they happen, it seems that if we do nothing they will all toddle off eventually. Half-Sister, who has been remarkably still of late, has informed me that she has found a novel way of witnessing her thoughts. The method she has invented involves imagining that thoughts are cats walking along the garden fence. When you want to let go of a thought, you just bat the cat off the fence and the thought is gone. This use of feline thought-patterns fits with Half-Sister's dislike of cats in general. She can smell them before you ever see them. Half-Sister and The Bookshelf had a conversation one afternoon about the difference between cats and dogs, and she later shared with me some remarkable facts. I am not sure if all the information is totally true, as I have a feeling some of it has been the subject of Half-Sister manipulation, however it's interesting all the same. A dog is a pack animal. A cat is a loner. Therefore, a cat is anti-social and not to be trusted. Dogs bark, growl, woof and use countless other noises to communicate. Cats just meow or purr, therefore they are uneducated. A dog scares away intruders. Cats just run away. Conclusion: they are cowards, hence the saying 'scaredy cats'. Dogs need lots of space to run around. Cats are happy in small spaces, so the best place for a cat is in a box. Eventually, we remember that we are supposed to be practicing the sitting meditation and, thanks to Awareness, get back to observing thoughts. That Wandering Mind is a tricky customer - sometimes she arrives through the back door.

Emotions

Let's not forget that the little emotions are the great captains of our lives, and we obey them without realizing it.

Vincent Van Gogh

The time we spent observing our thoughts has led us to believe that some thoughts may be connected to emotions. This seems to be felt not just in the mind, but also in the body. For instance, Half-Sister got very excited batting cats of the garden fence, and I noticed feelings of happiness and contentment at times, but at other times we were bored and restless. All this certainly produced sensations in the body; excitement created twitchiness, happiness produced snugglyness, and boredom made us restless and fidgety. Bearing all this in mind, we are now going to expand our attention to observing both thoughts and emotions, plus any sensations that happen to turn up. We would like to flag up at this point that the sitting meditation is now pushing spaniel observational skills to the limit, especially when you add Wandering Mind to the equation. Although we can handle it, we would just like to mention that this is *way* past the capabilities of the average cat. As Half-Sister points out, cats can't think outside the box. In the event of difficulties arising during the meditation, we are kindly reminded that we can use our wise choices. This includes using the breath as an anchor, moving up close to the difficulty, or leaving it just as it is.

Choiceless awareness

The ultimate value of life depends upon awareness and the power of contemplation, rather than upon mere survival.
Aristotle

In the remaining time, we are instructed to let go of all the objects we have been paying attention to, the breath, sensations in the body, sounds, thoughts and emotions. Instead, we are simply being aware of sitting here in the present moment. If thoughts pop into our head, we will observe them. If it's sounds then we will pay attention to sounds. If it's our breath we notice the most then we will be with the breath. Doing our best to be with arising experiences as they come and go. If Wandering Mind arrives, we will notice her (although Half-Sister will tell her to leg it as the bells are due any moment).

Upon reflection under the bamboo

It might be that the secret to spending more time in the present moment is to slow down just enough to have some awareness of what is actually happening in each moment, rather than zooming through each day. If we can accomplish that then we might be able to make wiser choices, and therefore live a more mindful and happy life. Everything that we experience, day-in, day-out, seems to influence how we feel and therefore how we get through the day. We think we have a great pal in the breath when it comes to staying in the present moment and not being influenced by Wandering Mind. The breath can be like an anchor holding a drifting ship, keeping us in the present moment rather than being lost in a sea of past and future thoughts. If we want to make wiser choices in life then we need to practice our meditation every day and develop our awareness. Half-Sister, who seems to have breezed through the sitting meditation, suggests we should go a step further and check in with the breath every time we remember. This will not only drop us into the present moment, but also reassure us we are still breathing, and therefore alive and kicking. She also advises that if you check in and there are no breaths, you should suspend the meditation practice and inform the vet ASAP. If you are a human being, you will need to join the queue at the hospital or take the faster option and pretend to be a dog with health insurance.

The human versions of the meditation practices can be found on www.garyheads.co.uk For all other dogs, please read this chapter and get your owner to download the practices.

5

Silent Retreat

In Mongolia, when a dog dies, he is buried high in the hills so people cannot walk on his grave. The dog's master whispers into the dog's ear his wishes that the dog will return as a man in his next life.

The Art of Racing in the Rain

Taking into account the stunning view out the window and all the current activity going on, I have decided to do a 'seeing meditation' as my morning practice.

Day 1

ALTHOUGH WE HAVE SEEN this strange activity before, we think it's safe to say that today is *definitely* not shaping up to be your average day. For a start, a lot of stuff is getting packed into the car as if we are moving house, including our food, which is a little disturbing. One thing that is for certain is that wherever that food is going, so is Half-Sister. If we are correct in our assumption, there will be no need to worry. After a short while we will be back home again. We think this activity is in preparation for something called a holiday (whatever that is). Mum and Dad don't go to work on these holidays. Instead, they just lounge about reading, going for walks and enjoying themselves. In the springer spaniel encyclopaedia, you can find this in the section called 'Life'.

Listening in to the pre-trip conversation, it sounds like we are off to a place called Dumfries and Galloway in Scotland. According to Mum, we are staying in a cottage that is in the middle of nowhere and has no Internet, mobile signal or TV. Half-Sister is mortified that there is no TV, but also slightly confused. No TV means there is no remote, yet in the brochure it said the cottage is very remote. Half-Sister's confusion is short-lived, however, as a more important conclusion has surfaced in her mind. If the holiday cottage is in the middle of nowhere, and mindfulness is a journey along a path that ultimately leads to nowhere, then we might just be heading in the right direction! The Bookshelf and I are not convinced of Half-Sister's theory, but at least it has taken her mind off the remote situation.

The journey is over three hours long and will be by far the longest time we have ever spent travelling in a car. That will be a new experience for both of us, as will sleeping in a cottage in Scotland. The car might be packed to the roof but there is still plenty of room for our beginner's minds, which should come in very handy as we really haven't been here before. All the books we have read so far have suggested that attending a silent retreat on a regular basis is an important part of meditation practice. This is obviously why Dad goes to a Buddhist monastery for his retreat each year. We have heard him tell Mum that there is no talking, no mobiles, TV or Internet, just sitting meditation and walking meditation all day long. There is also no food allowed after the mid-day meal. This has immediately got Half-Sister's attention, and I am unequivocally informed that if we are to turn our holiday into a silent retreat then she will be drawing a line under the absent-dinner situation. I have a feeling that if our retreat is to be a success, we will need to compromise around the food issue. Or have two breakfasts.

Weighing everything up, this seems to us like a perfect opportunity to embark on our first silent retreat. Perhaps a little bit of meditation in the morning, a little garden contemplation in the afternoon, and walking during the day. There will, of course, be no barking or howling allowed. Before any of that can take place, we first of all have to get there, and I have a history when it comes to travelling in a car. For the first hour or so I am usually fine, and then it starts. The panting, the slaver and finally, much to Half-Sister's disgust, my breakfast makes an appearance.

Despite everyone in the car praying, this trip was no different. Even with all my best efforts to just breath in and breath out, an hour into the journey and - whoosh! Everyone in the car knew it was coming. Dad was frantically looking for a stopping place, Mum had the paper towels ready, and Half-Sister was manoeuvring like a drunken belly-dancer. You could tell by the look in her eyes she knew it was going to blow, and it surely did.

Now, as we all know, the mind can be a funny thing, *especially* when it comes to worrying about the past or predicting the future. You can tell by the expression on Dad's face that he is thinking about stopping every so often in an attempt to avoid further episodes of pukey-ness. Mum, on the other hand, is definitely still on red alert with the paper towels, whilst Half-Sister is wedged in the corner, trying to work out potential lines of fire and where the best place is to sit to avoid the possibility of her first Scottish bath. Me, I am asleep, and I stay that way until we get there.

Eventually we arrive at our destination, much to the relief of all concerned. While everything is getting unpacked and taken into our temporary home, we begin to think about the word remote. It is an interesting word to contemplate. At home, remote means switching on the entertainment on the television. Here, it appears to mean something very similar, only the entertainment in this instance is the Scottish countryside. As the unpacking continues, we are allowed to play in the huge back garden. The first thing we notice upon skidding onto the lawn is the multitude of smells, far too many for two small noses to take in all at once. It's all very exciting, so I decide to go off exploring with Beginner's Mind and Curiosity in tow. Meanwhile, Half-Sister is attempting to count how many different shades of green she can find in the garden. After using up all her toes she decides to give up, and instead launches herself into the bushes and undergrowth. She returns after a short while looking remarkably like the plant department at Ikea. We have only been here a short while, but have already acquired the taste for retreats. Perhaps if we are good Dad might take us with him the next time he goes. One thing we have noticed is that staying in the present moment is much easier when you are somewhere as interesting as this. I wonder, if we lived here all the time, would we slip into automatic pilot and take it all for granted? That's a sad thought.

After we have all settled into our new surroundings, it's time for an exploratory stroll in the rain with Dad. Half-Sister is helping mum unpack the food as she is not keen on rain. At the beginning of our walk I find myself slipping into my usual striving mode. Eagerness begins to take over as I yearn to find out where we are going. When I do this I am always made to stop and start again. This happens over and over until I eventually learn to take my time and walk at the same speed as Dad, which is usually one gear up from 'happy wander'. Eventually, we match our steps and fall into a rhythm. All of a sudden something clicks in my mind, and I realise that striving to get to the next place, or around the next corner, means I miss the journey. I never quite arrive in the moment. As I have not been here before, every step is a step into the unknown. Plus, Dad, having not been here before either, hasn't a clue where he is going anyway.

If you remember, you can turn walking outside into one big meditation. It's all about paying attention and being aware of what is around you. There are so many smells, sounds, sights and sensations to notice that your walk can be transformed into a mini nature programme. Half-Sister might be working on her 'fifty shades of green' meditation, but I am going to make a note of how many different beings I can notice on this walk, apart from the human one next to me and myself of the canine variety. Now, where I live, the squirrels are grey. We used to have the red variety, but the grey ones launched a successful takeover bid. Here in the Scottish countryside, there are red squirrels in abundance. I think they are rather pretty. Perhaps we could take some back with us and repopulate the forest at the back of our house, a bit like the environmental folks did with the red kites. Now, the red kites where we live are smart. They have worked out that rather than flying in circles looking for dead stuff in the fields, it's *much* more productive to fly in circles over the supermarket in the village. I like their style. Half-Sister, having finished supervising the food storage, has now joined us and is being most helpful in identifying the flying variety of beings in this meditation. This is mainly due to her discovering that the big poster in the cottage is, in fact, a who's who of the bird variety and not a menu as she first thought.

Here, for all those of a bird-watching disposition, are the details of our observations so far, plus a few queries:

A Great-spotted woodpecker (as opposed to an okay spotted woodpecker?)

Nuthatch

Robin

Sparrow

Chaffinch

Great tit (same question applies as above)

Coal tit

And, speak of the devil, our old pal the red kite.

There he was, circling the skies, looking for dead stuff in the fields, totally oblivious to the fact that only five miles down the road there is a supermarket. All the above were noticed by simply being mindful and paying attention on our walk. It's a good list. If you are wondering about the queries, they are yet to be resolved.

When we get back to the cottage, everything appears to be in order and we are set for the evening. Half-Sister, who disappeared halfway through the walk, has returned from the undergrowth and has brought home a million spiky burrs as a memento. Mum is attempting to pick and brush them out; however Half-Sister, who has never been keen on being brushed, has returned to her drunken-belly dancer moves in the hope that Mum will give up. Who wins this battle of wills is open to debate.

Once evening arrives, the contentious subject of

sleeping arrangements arises. At home this would be plain-sailing. I sleep downstairs on the rocky chair in the kitchen, and Half-Sister sleeps upstairs on the landing. Simple. Everything as it should be. However, when we are staying away from home it's a free-for-all, and everywhere is up for grabs. Before a successful outcome can be achieved, you need to become familiar with the 'how to get your own way' techniques. These are inbred in springer spaniels, and come in handy in a situation such as this. At the risk of giving away spaniel trade secrets, we will explain further. The issue to be addressed - everyone is sleeping in the bedroom apart from us. Our intention - we want in.

If we were at home, the following technique would not work, but here in our holiday cottage there is a subtle difference: this is not our house. At the beginning of the holiday booking process, just as Mum was about to reserve the cottage, she noticed at the bottom of the form the following statement: 'Dogs are welcome.' However, underneath in small print it also said, 'Do you want to insure against damage?'. Mum looked down at me, just as my best angelic face peered up at her. She smiled and thought, 'No, they will be fine.' Just at the moment the pen ticked the 'no' box, Half-Sister skidded into the kitchen with the TV remote in her mouth. She was accompanied by her well-practiced evil grin and had the timing of a master manipulator. Now we have the insurance issue sorted, which was an important part of the plan. I provided the reassurance that everything would be fine, Half-Sister provided the doubt. Furthermore, Mum has now moved in her mind to 'What if' syndrome. This is a key element to successfully getting your own way. We will explain further. Having made the decision to opt out of the accidental damage insurance, we now need Mum to produce thoughts in her mind about all the things that could possibly go wrong involving us spaniels. We also need her to recall all the dodgy stuff we have done in the past, just to emphasis the point. Half-Sister's timely appearance took care of that one. Now the slightest suggestion that we are up to no good and her buttons will get pressed - she will get anxious and give in to our demands.

Fast-forward to bedtime. They are in the bedroom. We are not. However, Mum is yet to go to sleep. She is probably mulling over potential problems and wondering if we are asleep. Perfect. Like two master safe-crackers, we weigh up the situation. Half-Sister gives the signal and I step aside, as she is the master and I am only the apprentice. The cunning plan starts with a very subtle, low-pitched whine, just enough to let her know we are outside the door and awake. This starts her thinking. All it takes after that is two scrats at the carpet and one howl of the banshee and we are in. Easy really. I like sleeping under the bed. Half-Sister prefers to stretch out in the middle of the bed like the Queen of Sheba (whoever she is). Now that we are all comfy and warm, Half-Sister has decided to read a poem she has found in the cottage to end the day. It goes with her shades of green meditation:

> Stand tall and proud
> Go out on a limb
> Remember your roots
> Drink plenty of water
> Be content with your natural beauty
> Enjoy the view
>
> *Advice from a tree*

Day 2

We are awoken from our slumber by the pitter-patter of rain on the window and the sound of the birds, as there is a bird feeder right outside the bedroom window. Dad took care to fill it up yesterday evening but, judging by the racket outside, he will need a lorry delivery of birdseed to keep these guys fed for the next week. Taking into account the stunning view *out the window* and all the current activity going on, I have decided to do a 'seeing meditation' as my morning practice. I allow myself a little time to settle in before focusing my attention on the birdfeeder outside and beginning to notice things unfolding moment-by-moment. As instructed by the numerous meditation teachers (including Dad) that have permeated my ears, I remember that if my mind wanders, especially to thoughts about breakfast, I will just bring it back to noticing. All the birds from yesterday's list make an appearance, apart from the red kite that is. If that guy turns up, everyone in the house will be awake. We have new visitors too, including a field mouse, a vole and a big fat rat. Now, I know we are supposed to bring non-judgemental thinking to our meditation practice, but I have noticed that my thoughts about the rat are different to the thoughts arising about the other creatures. In other words, I don't like 'em. Dad suggests it's good to practice with things we don't like, so bearing that in mind I reluctantly send kind and compassionate thoughts towards the rat and the rest of his family, who have just turned up to the party.

My morning meditation is proving to be a fascinating experience and is unfolding in so many interesting ways. The thing that has attracted my attention the most is the wonder of nature in action, an example of this being in the food distribution department. A red squirrel arrives and, in its excitement, sends seeds and peanuts flying all over the place. Due to this action, the robin, mouse and rat family look down at the earth and think it's Christmas. As they couldn't reach the nuts before, thanks to the red squirrel everybody is now happy and will soon be stuffed full. Talking about things arriving, I have just noticed that Half-Sister has joined me. She is yet to have her breakfast and is looking out the window as if the birdfeeder has manifested into the local takeaway. Time to wake up Dad I think.

Throughout the rest of the day we continue to take walks in the beautiful countryside, the only dampener being all the rain that has decided to accompany us on our way. Half-Sister has been paying attention and has noticed that when it's raining, the ferns, plants and trees seem to get brighter, as if someone has just plugged them in and switched them on. She has also noticed that when the rain drips from the trees onto the big ferns, the ferns look as if they are dancing. I think she is right on this one, just like she was right about the puddle water being nicer to drink than the tap variety. As the day progresses, we fall into our retreat routine: walking meditation, sleeping meditation, walking meditation, sleeping meditation, eating meditation, sleeping meditation. You get the picture. When evening arrives, Mum doesn't even consider shutting us out of the bedroom. Due to the conditioned nature of human beings, and Half-Sister's psychological adeptness, she is now completely programmed and on automatic pilot. She might as well give us the blankets and hot water bottles now.

Day 3

Today, much to our surprise, the sun has decided to make an appearance. This has resulted in all the puddles disappearing and everything looking colourful but less shiny. The rain made everything bright, but today it looks like everybody has switched to energy saving light bulbs. During the course of the day it stays mostly sunny, apart from the odd power cut when everything goes dark for a while and the rain pays us a quick visit. Half-Sister is unfortunately suffering from withdrawal symptoms today and has taken to substituting her missing TV remote for a big stone that was being used to prop open the door to the utility room in the cottage. The trouble is every time she picks it up she has to be rescued, as the door shuts behind her and locks her in the utility. She is not having a good day. Now, the fact that difficulties are arising today fits in with what Dad told Mum about when he goes on silent retreats. He reckons that about half way through you can have a bit of a wobble and want to go home, but after a while you get over it and could stay for weeks. I suppose all that meditation practice, reflection and non-talking might be a bit unsettling after a while. On the positive side what better opportunity to unravel the workings of the mind and investigate the conditioning you may have picked up since childhood/puppyhood. You might even discover insightful moments that lead to enlightenment or, as suggested by Half-Sister, you could just drop the big stone and storm off in a huff.

Day 4

After one day of sunshine, the rain is back again. This development seems to have delighted the ferns, who are once again partying and dancing. On our soggy walks today, I have taken the opportunity to partake in a bit of contemplating. Rainy walks can be good for this, plus it takes your mind off the fact that you are soaking wet. One thing that has popped into my mind is that, apart from the lady who owns the cottage, we have yet to meet another human being so far on this holiday/retreat, or another dog for that matter. It's just been me and Mum, Dad and our thoughts, with an occasional visit from Half-Sister in between huffs. All this reflection has gotten me thinking about thoughts, and especially where they come from. It's weird how they just arrive and drop in without an invitation.

Furthermore, I have noticed that if you want to get rid of a thought, it might go away but then it sometimes comes back with all its mates in tow. This usually results in all hell breaking loose.

So today, in keeping with the contemplating thoughts theme, my meditation practice has been all about observing thoughts. Not for too long mind, as you could end up thinking you are barking mad if you keep it up all day. I have to report that so far the practice has produced lots of thoughts about thoughts, and thoughts about observing thoughts. See, you have to be careful with all this stuff or you could think yourself loopy.

To avoid verging on over-pondering all this, I am taking a moment to recall the theory shared by The Bookshelf last week. If I remember it correctly, the theory goes something like this. Thoughts are not facts, not even the tricky ones that tell you they are. And you are not your thoughts. 'So what are the little blighters then you might ask?' They are simply mental events that pop into your head, and then skedaddle off again.

Thoughts arise and pass like clouds in the sky, or squirrels up a tree, or in Half-Sister's case, TV channels with a bite of the remote. Some come around more than once, especially thoughts about walks or food. Some can be scary, and surprise you when you least expect it. The Bookshelf told me that it's not thoughts that cause the problems, but what we choose to do with them. There are thoughts that make us feel happy, whilst some make us sad, and others that we don't care about at all. I'm keeping an eye on mine because, due to all these thoughts arising, I have forgotten about my lovely walk and the dancing ferns. I think it's time to pay attention.

Day 5

The Buddha informs us that we suffer because we want things to be different from how they are. Darn right. I am sick of smelling like a mouldy carpet due to all this rain. However, the inclement weather won't stop Dad from taking us walking and exploring, and it won't stop the ferns from their partying and boogying either. As if to validate yesterday's meditation regarding thoughts coming and going, all references to mouldy carpets and soggy smells evaporate in an instant as the rain suddenly stops. Impermanence - nothing lasts forever and a lesson in patience, so contrary to all previous thoughts I only smell of springer spaniel. It seems that Half-Sister's bad mood is also subject to impermanence because she has now joined us on the walk accompanied by Mum. It's sad to think that everything is impermanent, but it's also a timely reminder that we should remember to pay attention to what is happening right now and enjoy the moment. Currently, Half-Sister is in full-striving mode and wants, as usual, to be in front on the walk. As she is built like a hairy bulldozer, there is no stopping her. Mum, who has Half-Sister on a lead, is getting pulled along too and is in danger of becoming impermanent. We all get told off, including me for joining in the imaginary race and Dad for laughing. In the grand scheme of things, our telling-off is also impermanent, so we decide we might as well do it all over again.

Day 6

This is our last full day before we make the journey home. It's also the last day of sleeping in the bedroom. Even luxury is impermanent it seems. Other examples of impermanence are that all the leaves are falling off the trees due to the current high winds, and that most of the food has disappeared. This has resulted in Dad having to venture into the nearest town to stock up. On food, by the way, not leaves. It's a five-mile trek to the nearest supermarket and we can only hope that our old pal the red kite decides to follows him out of curiosity.

All this time we have spent in the countryside meditating and reflecting in silence has resulted in Half-Sister going all contemplative on me today. This might be partly due to a book about Karma and reincarnation falling out of the bookcase (no relation) in the cottage and landing on her head. Without the distraction of stealing the TV remote, she has over pondered the subject. The following is the theory of Karma and reincarnation according to Half-Sister. If we do good things, good things will come our way, but if we do dodgy stuff, things will not turn out well. On top of this, when we are reincarnated we could come back as anything. What we are reincarnated as is determined not only by our actions in this life, but previous ones as well. Half-Sister has been totting up all the dodgy stuff she has done over the years and thinks things are not looking too good. Currently its 5/4 on being reincarnated as a dung beetle, and 13/8 as a cat, with the odds changing by the moment. Taking everything into consideration, she thinks that there is no time to waste and is turning over a new leaf. It's *definitely* damage limitation time. Half-Sister is obviously taking this reincarnation business very seriously, because on our next walk she is walking like one of those Cruft's posers - not one bit of striving. This has amazed Mum, who keeps looking down as the lead is so slack she thinks Half-Sister must have legged it. Later in the evening, she gives Mum the big stone from the utility as a present. Mum is visibly shocked at this development and cracks open the wine.

Now, Half-Sister did do her best to explain the complexities of Karma and reincarnation, but I can't help but think that her efforts to rectify the situation may have backfired on her. I overheard Mum and Dad discussing how she is acting weird and will need to go to the vet when we get back (the psychology department no less). Apparently, Half-Sister might need CBT (Canine Behavioural Therapy). Payback time indeed!

Evidently, you need to have done a lot of good deeds to be reincarnated as a human being. Unfortunately there is no mention in the Karma book of spaniel deeds and how that pans out. Maybe it works in reverse, because when Dad looks at us all stretched out on the sofa warm and cosy and he is going off to work in the cold, he often says he is coming back as a springer spaniel. Now that would be fun!

Day 7

It's packing-up-and-going-home day today, but before we do that there is still enough time for one last walk in the lovely Scottish countryside. In the spirit of our silent retreat, we are being mindful of our surroundings whilst tuning in to our paws touching the ground as we walk. As it's the last day, barking is now allowed. All the creatures that live here are in evidence and we are thanking them for sharing their home with us for a week. This even includes the rats and especially the red kite, although we have no idea if he ever found the supermarket. We had ticked all the birds on the poster in the kitchen apart from one, but today we are pleased to report it arrived in all its splendour - a beautiful jay. This has been our practice this morning - gratitude. It is so easy to forget all the things in life that we should be grateful for. I guess that's something else we go on automatic pilot with. Half-Sister is grateful she is a springer spaniel and informs me that she would be very grateful if I didn't throw up on the way home. I am grateful that she is my Half-Sister, but I can't promise her the other request.

Upon reflection under the bamboo

Now that we are back home and have had time to reflect upon our silent retreat experience, the following conclusions have been unanimously agreed upon. It occurs to us that we may have an inner-life and an outer-life, and that the inner life influences how we view the outer one. On our retreat we did our meditation every day, and noticed that this helped us to slow down and pay attention to what was happening in our minds and bodies. However, our practice expanded into our outer life and made the experience more interesting, which made us happy. This is only a spaniel's view, and so no responsibility is taken for a human being's experience of a silent retreat. Half-Sister has also pondered the benefits of the silent retreat and has come up with the following observations. We definitely learnt to appreciate nature and spend quality time with our owners. It was also good for recharging our batteries and quieting the little lady, Wandering Mind. As our cottage didn't have a TV, we walked more, played more and explored the environment. We spent more time in the present moment and so noticed and enjoyed our holiday/retreat all the more.

PS
Dad has just returned from the garage due to a strange noise the car was making all the way home. We are happy to report that the car is fine, although they did present him with a bill. And a large stone.

There is more to life than a TV remote and running in circles.

Half-Sister

6

Reincarnation – I'm sure we have been here before

We all have some experience of a feeling that comes over us occasionally, of what we are saying and doing having been said and done before, in a remote time - of our having been surrounded, dim ages ago, by the same faces, objects, and circumstances.

Charles Dickens

As there now seems to be an interlude in proceedings due to Half-Sister's science lesson, I have decided to go for a wander in the garden with my old pal the tennis ball.

AFTER THE ARISING OF Half-Sister's spontaneous insight that manifested itself due to the reincarnation and Karma book landing on her head, we thought it would be wise to look into the subject in more detail, starting with the issue of reincarnation.

Before we reflect upon what the Buddha said about the subject, we should perhaps first listen to the words uttered by Half-Sister as she stood at the top of the stairs this morning. It is obvious that the effects of her head trauma are yet to recede.

"Every morning, when you open your eyes, you have the opportunity to reincarnate into a better and wiser spaniel, if you remember to make the effort." Where does she get this stuff from? After this early morning sermon, it was time to charge down the stairs and bark for breakfast. No change there then.

It is said and confirmed by The Bookshelf, the keeper of our in-house library to give him his full title, that the Buddha left 84,000 teachings. The Buddha's teachings were suitable for all, from a poor beggar to a wealthy king; however, there is still no mention of teachings specifically for dogs. Bearing this in mind, you now have a choice. You can leg it to the library and flick through the 84,000 teachings and make your own mind up about reincarnation, or you can continue reading this chapter and get the springer spaniel version. The choice is yours.

After breakfast has been served, Half-Sister, who has awoken in a very philosophical and thought-provoking mood, proceeds to tell me that she is not the same spaniel that she was when she was born, or the same spaniel as last year, or even last night. Intrigued by this, I ask her to explain further, as even The Bookshelf looks confused. She does look to us like the Half-Sister of yesterday, but I have to say she is definitely not behaving as per the usual Half-Sister remit.

The Bookshelf and I settle in as Half-Sister proceeds to tell us that although at first this was all very confusing, the hours of pondering under the bamboo has paid dividends. According to the theory, it appears that human beings are *constantly* being reborn. This is because their cells are constantly changing to new ones. Even though they might think they are the same, they are in fact not the same human being that they were last night, last week or last month. This is like the universe, every atom and molecule constantly changing, recycling, and reborn. As we are all children of the universe, it must therefore be the same for us springer spaniels. So, to reaffirm my previous statement, I am not the same spaniel that was born in the Lake District; I am not the same spaniel as last year, or even last night, and tomorrow I will be reborn yet again. With these words, she trots off to the kitchen, leaving The Bookshelf and I practicing our best frowns. After several minutes, the silence is eventually broken when The Bookshelf frantically announces the following: "Let's get on Amazon - we need new books and fast."

Several days later, the Amazon man struggles up the steps with a huge box. The box includes books on quantum physics, the universe, rebirth, and woodwork. It seems like The Bookshelf has taken Half-Sister's theory to heart and is currently too busy to talk to us.

As there now seems to be an interlude in proceedings due to Half-Sister's science lesson, I have decided to go for a wander in the garden with my old pal the tennis ball. The bamboo is currently empty, so what better time to embark on a ponder. I am just observing Half-Sister at the far end of the garden recycling her breakfast when it hits me - literally - on the head. A leaf - a very pretty orange one, although I have noticed they don't stay that colour for long. It has fallen off the tree because it's time for it to go. It will eventually go squidgy, and then disappear into the earth where it originally came from. Come the spring it will be back again, reborn. It's the law of nature. It may look different, but in essence it's still a leaf.

After all that contemplation, it's time for a snooze under the bamboo. I am just about to close my eyes when I catch Half-Sister winking at me. Interesting.

Several weeks later, The Bookshelf finally emerges from his self-imposed exile and proclaims that he hopes he comes back as a library and not as a garden shed. He thinks he should be fine because he has done nothing but support things all his life. We will leave him with that one.

Anyway, back to what the Buddha said about all this reincarnation/rebirth business. Well for starters, the news looks bleak. In fact it seems like we are all doomed to extermination. However, rather than get all despondent about things, we should simply regard it as a natural part of the process of birth, old age and death. We should always keep in mind the impermanence of life, just like my leaf. Remember, this is not the end of life, just the end of the body. The spirit remains, and we will get a new body and a new life. What kind of body and life we end up with is down to Karma, and will be determined by the results of our past actions. We should not fear the end because we will be back in one form or another.

Half-Sister, who has been very quiet, suddenly announces from the top of the stairs her take on the above:

"We are all gonna cop it sooner or later, so it's no use expecting otherwise. But, we will be back because it's only temporary. The question is what do we come back as? That is in the lap of the gods (Karma)."

In the Buddhist texts it is said that on the night the Buddha became enlightened, he gained the ability to recall all his previous lives, even the details of his name and profession. That's a cool trick, especially as he is said to have recalled an endless amount. Hearing this, Half-Sister is now concerned about cats, especially the ginger one next door and his feline pals. She thinks they could be pulling a fast-one here. As they are supposed to have nine lives to start with, how does that work in terms of reincarnation? This revelation has done nothing for Half-Sister's attitude towards cats, as she now thinks they should not be trusted, even when they are dead. While we are on the subject of cool tricks and cats, there is also the fact that they always land on their feet. That's not normal is it? If only the Buddha was still around to look into this, or Right Nuisance, who would have known. The Buddha also said that we don't necessarily have to believe in rebirth to practice his teachings, although we are thinking that if he said it, we believe him. This fits nicely with his statement that we should question everything until we truly believe it for ourselves. A wise man indeed.

Moving on from the Buddha's questioning advice to The Bookshelf, who is now trying to explain to us the *Quantum Theory of Consciousness*. According to the theory, our consciousness, or mind, exists as a sphere beyond our perceived three-dimensional reality. This statement, rather than encouraging curiosity and interest, only succeeds in creating a very large frown from Half-Sister, followed by a huge yawn. Unperturbed, The Bookshelf cracks on. Our body receives a transmission, like a radio signal from a broadcaster. These transmissions are our thoughts, feelings and mental images. To us they appear to be occurring in the body, but this is like saying all the music is stored in the radio. So everything is not actually in our head, but rather comes from the realm where the mind is located. Half-Sister, who has been listening intently to The Bookshelf's explanation, suddenly chirps up that she knew this all along. This prior knowledge is evidently due to the fact that she sometimes listens to the football with Dad on a tiny radio. In the words of Half-Sister, it's all very simple really. How could you possibly get 52,000 fans, two teams, a ref, a ball and all those half-time pints of beer, not to mention the pies, in that tiny radio? Therefore the commentary must come from somewhere else. Before The Bookshelf can enthusiastically continue, Half-Sister summarises. The radio breaks, but the match continues on. We get a new radio and tune back in to the football. The body dies but the signal continues broadcasting - we get a new body and bingo. We are back in business!

Much to The Bookshelf's disappointment, this seems to be the end of the conversation. A springer spaniel's break-neck-speed tour of quantum theory. As per the Buddha's instructions, I would suggest you question this explanation thoroughly.

Half-Sister's plan to stockpile good Karma, instigated in her case to avoid spending time on cat duties in the future, appears to have been a good move. If we concur with the Buddhist view, we could pop up in any one of six different realms. These realms all have strange-sounding names, which The Bookshelf has kindly translated using the Teach Yourself Pali book Dad bought but gave up trying to use. Pali is an ancient language spoken in the Buddha's time. To begin with, there is the **Deva** (heavenly) realm, where different types of non-human beings hang out. They are more powerful, live longer and are generally happier than human beings. Interesting. Us spaniels are non-human, and generally happier. That must be why we can be a bit diva-ish at times. Then there is the **Asura** (demigod) realm, which seems to us to be a very scary realm. Asuras are described as having three heads with three faces each, and either four or six arms. Enough said about that lot. Moving on to the next realm, we have **Manusya** (human). Manusya is a very special status, as humans can achieve enlightenment. However, in Buddhism, humans are just one type of sentient being. In other words, a being with a mind stream. The next one is us - **Tiryak** (animals). Animals inhabit the great oceans or live mostly on the earth. They live in water, trees, or in our case, in the house (especially on the sofa). The realm of **Preta** (ghosts), which is next on the list, seems even scarier than that lot, with a multitude of heads, faces, and arms. These beings are supernatural, and have endured more suffering than humans, especially, in terms of levels of hunger and thirst. In fact, they are called 'hungry ghosts' in English. How they ended up here is all down to being false, corrupted, compulsive, deceitful, jealous or greedy people in a previous life. As a result, they have an insatiable hunger for a particular substance or object. Just imagine every day is Halloween, but you can never get enough chocolate. They are also invisible to the human eye, and are described as human-like but with mummified skin, narrow limbs, enormous distended bellies and long, thin necks. They are always, hungry hence the big belly, but can't satisfy their hunger, so a long, thin neck. Yuck. Maybe something like a cross between a giraffe and a pregnant orangutan. There will be a name for this combination, but it escapes us. We could always consult the sprocker who lives down by the river - she is our resident canine combination expert as she is half-cocker spaniel and half-springer spaniel.

Finally we come to the last realm, which is **Naraka** (resident of hell). Being born here is a direct result of accumulated actions (Karma), and you stay here for an incomprehensibly long time - in fact, hundreds of millions of years. Eventually you will be re-born higher up the ladder, but it obviously takes a *very* long time. A bit like our Dad's wait for his football team to win a cup.

As this is a complicated subject, here is our best shot at clarifying our findings. Rebirth is determined by Karma; good realms are favoured by good Karma and rebirth in the dodgy evil realms is the consequence of bad Karma. Although enlightenment is the end goal, we also need to get some good Karma in the bank to avoid being reborn in one of the evil realms.

Having listened very carefully to all this, Half-Sister has decided that being reborn as a cat might actually be a result. Anything has got to be better than coming back as a giraffytan and always being thirsty and hungry.

You are feeling sleepy, very sleepy

Now, in keeping with the Buddha's suggestion that we should question everything, we are now endeavouring to unravel the whole reincarnation theory by exploring the evidence-base. This is of particular interest to Half-Sister, given her theory about potentially being the reincarnated spaniel previously known as Right Nuisance.

After an intensive search, The Bookshelf has come up with an article called '*The Science of Reincarnation*'. Sounds promising. It turns out that, according to the article, some people appear to remember previous lives. Interestingly, many of the examples involve children, such as the five-year-old boy that remembered dying in a fire, or the twin girls recalling being killed in a car crash. There was even a suggestion that a grandad had been reborn as his grandson. Some people even had the same birthmarks as the life before. Although all this is fascinating, it poses more questions than answers, so we keep searching.

After a while, The Bookshelf begins to shake. This is always a sign that he has found something of great interest. This is then followed by a short pause, as if he is internally debating whether he should actually share his findings or not. Eventually he rather hesitantly proclaims that he is going to hypnotise Half-Sister. When her growling and circle-turning subsides, he explains further. It turns out that there is something called *Past Life Regression*. It's a technique that therapists use to hypnotise people and regress them back to previous lives. The Bookshelf reckons it will be no problem after reading the book. Let's face it, how hard can it be, and what's the worst that can happen?

Two days later, the contents of the book have been absorbed and The Bookshelf is ready to give it a go. Timing is everything, so he has chosen after dinnertime to perform the therapeutic task. Half-Sister will hopefully be sleepy and perhaps less resistant to the process, although she is eager to find out about her past lives. Due to Half-Sister's vast knowledge of films and programmes acquired through the TV remote, she has asked if we are using a dangly pocket watch. She has seen this done in a film a while ago, where a lady was hypnotised using this method and then started talking in Japanese. The Bookshelf assures us that we are not using a dangly pocket watch on this occasion, although we do think there is one in the house somewhere. That's a shame - Mum's face would have been a treat when Half-Sister started barking for her tea in Japanese. It would have been a classic moment in our lives.

Eventually, we are all gathered in the dining room and ready to begin the *Past Life Regression*. Half-Sister looks slightly anxious and not adverse to the odd spin. The Bookshelf tells her to make herself comfortable, so in true Half-Sister fashion, she drops into an undignified posture. I am not sure that was what he had in mind, but it's too late now.

The Bookshelf, using his *Past Life Regression* book for guidance, begins the process of hypnotising Half-Sister. He starts by ringing Dad's meditation bells that we discovered in his office. Three dings of the bell signify that we have begun. The sound of the bell has hardly subsided before it is swiftly followed by the words, 'You are beginning to feel sleepy and your body feels very heavy.' The Bookshelf is keen. Looking at Half-Sister, this stuff works remarkably fast, especially as The Bookshelf is a novice in this area. Due to the dramatic speed of progress, we skip the next few pages and go straight to the nitty-gritty. He tells her to imagine that she is falling down a well and that the well is all her past lives. He encourages her to notice the different stages of the journey and who she is, as she goes deeper and deeper into the well. Now, this all sounds very impressive, but I can't help but notice that The Bookshelf is not referring to the book anymore. He either has a good memory or he is making all this stuff up. Either way, Half-Sister is zonked out and we are enjoying ourselves, so we crack on regardless.

After about ten minutes, The Bookshelf suddenly announces that there is a slight problem, although slight might not be the right word. We have somehow veered off the hypnosis track due to over enthusiasm, and gotten lost in our imagination. The result of all this is that we are now unsure how to end the session. What we are really saying here is that we don't know how to stop Half-Sister flying down the well, presumably as herself and a variety of other creations. We can only hope one of them is a bird. Finally, after a long discussion around options, we plump for simplicity and The Bookshelf utters the following: "You have now reached the bottom of the well." Gingerly, The Bookshelf sounds the bells three times and then stands back like a small child on bonfire night. Half-Sister is unmoving, apart from the odd snore and the occasional twitch. Eventually, after what seems like an age, she opens one eye and The Bookshelf breathes a sigh of relief. As soon as she flips from her undignified posture to all fours, we start the interrogation. This, however, is to no avail, as Half-Sister immediately turns and heads for the kitchen for a drink of water. We watch eagerly as the water disappears at the usual rate of knots. Obviously *Past Life Regression* is a thirsty business. Finally, The Bookshelf can wait no longer and launches into an investigation any TV detective would have been proud to instigate. Unfortunately it appears that Half-Sister has been well-briefed by her reincarnation solicitor, and simply replies, 'No comment.' The only information she shares with us is that she awoke with a shudder, and for some reason she has a sore head. The Bookshelf decides it might be best to leave it at that.

Upon reflection under the bamboo

We have decided that this shall be a relatively short reflection under the bamboo. This is mainly due to not wanting to over-ponder the scary stuff around reincarnation and the various realms you can end up in. To simplify matters, we think it would be advisable if we all did our best to be good, therefore accumulating the Karma essential to coming back as something that's acceptable, and preferably in a place that is not over-populated with long-necked, fat-bellied thingamajigs. If Half-Sister discovered anything from her *Past Life Regression* experience, she is keeping it to herself. Personally I think she just had an afternoon nap, although the waking up with a sore head requires further investigation. The Bookshelf is currently reluctant to tackle that one. Who knows - perhaps one day we will discover the outcome of the wooden one's therapy. I think it is highly unlikely that we will be allowed to try it again.

7
Karma – we have been good, honest

Karma is like a rubber band - you can only stretch it so far before it comes back and smacks you in the face.

Anon

Today it is raining, and it looks like one of those days where it will rain all day, just because it can and basically feels like it.

TAKING EVERYTHING INTO ACCOUNT, it seems that Karma is *very* important if we are to progress on our journey to enlightenment. Unfortunately it also appears to be a tricky and complicated subject to get your head around. However, in true spaniel fashion we are doing our best to unravel it, albeit with a bit of help from The Bookshelf, Google and a couple of wet and curious noses. We began with the dictionary which said that Karma, according to Hinduism and Buddhism, is the sum of a person's actions in this and previous states of existence, and is viewed as deciding their fate in future existences. By pure coincidence, we also discovered that the Sanskrit word Karma means action, Sanskrit being an ancient human language. While we had our heads in the dictionary, we also unearthed the Sanskrit word for dog, which turns out to be Shvan. Half-Sister has just informed me that in spanialism, Karma means 'do good things and all will be well, be naughty and a ton of poo will land on your head sometime in the future.'

Not knowing anything about Karma is seemingly no excuse - if you get out of line the poo will eventually arrive. This seems a bit like putting stuff on your Amazon-wish list; it stays there for ages and looks like nothing is happening, then surprise! Somebody sends it. After intense pondering (bordering on a headache), we concluded the following: *The Law of Karma*, simply, you reap what you sow and this extends from past lives into future lives. How you stick to this law determines what happens in the future. So you need to be mindful of your actions, or it will either be raining buttercups and daisies, or something similar to when Half-Sister ate the dodgy plant in the garden and turned into the Wookie from Star Wars before unleashing. Need I go on?

Whilst searching the Internet, we came across the following poem about Karma. Seems appropriate as we know lots of ants. I think we have underestimated their importance, as they obviously have a significant role to play besides circle-dancing.

Lesson of time

When a bird is alive... it eats ants
When the bird is dead...ants eat the bird
Time and Circumstances can change at any time
Don't devalue or hurt anyone in this life
You may be powerful today. But remember
Time is more powerful than you
One tree makes a million match sticks
Only one matchstick is needed to burn a million trees
So be good and do good.

Unknown

We have realised from the previous chapter about reincarnation that not paying attention to your actions can land you in some right dodgy places. This includes realms where creatures with multiple faces and limbs hang out, not to mention the hungry ghosts - even the Amazon man couldn't deliver enough grub to satisfy their giant bellies! Taking all this into consideration, it stands to reason that we should look to uncover exactly what constitutes good Karma so we can avoid these evil realms. It seems a no-brainer to us that keeping to the Buddha's *five precepts* would create good Karma. It also appears that the potential to fall off the karmic wagon is possible in every waking moment. It's quite a responsibility, this idea of cause and effect, action and reaction, but you can only do your best with your actions and deeds. However, if we have the intention to work at it, we can help create a more beautiful and kindly world. What better reason than that to get stuck in!

How do we practice good karma?

The general consensus is that whatever happens in our lives is a reaction to our own previous actions - it's an effect of what we've done. All our intentional actions have an effect, so we are basically going along creating our reality through our Karma. I wonder what intentional act sent my tennis ball flying into the woods, lost forever, game over? Half-Sister and I are in agreement that it is all about doing good deeds and taking wise action. Not just us, but everyone else too, and it should also include taking care of the planet and everything on it. Half-Sister is advocating that we think of our lives as being like the back garden. It's big and you can run around at full speed. It also has the additional bonus of backing onto the woods. Because we like it so much, we take great care of it; Dad cuts the grass every two weeks and the poo-pickers are out on a regular basis.

With time and effort, it is a beautiful space. In spite of all this effort, we do need to realize that some things in the garden are beyond our control. This includes the weather, changing seasons, other animals visiting and people walking on it. We might ultimately determine what our garden looks like, but it's also up to us how we react to the imperfect bits and the arrival of the unexpected. Talking about the unexpected and reactions, the ginger one next door has just dropped into the garden. The explanation is suspended for the moment as Half-Sister rolls up her fur and skids out the back door. The Bookshelf and I peer out the window to witness the spectacle and to see Karma being created before our very eyes.

After serious consideration, we have decided that the best course of action on our karmic quest is to set an intention to cultivate mindfulness and compassion on a daily basis. We will also do our best to look after our family, the environment and ourselves. This will include spending as much time as possible in nature. If we endeavour to find the joy in the small things in life, study, and listen carefully, we will give ourselves the best chance of developing wisdom. It is our intention to build good Karma by replacing anger, greed and negativity with love and kindness, thereby staying on the right side of the karmic fence. Just as the echoes of that sentence reverberate, back comes Half-Sister, fresh from chasing the ginger one next door a million times around the garden. After listening to a summary of the good Karma plan of action, she looks me straight in the eye and says, "Great, it's a plan. Count me in." She then scuttles back outside at a rate of knots, her last words ringing around the kitchen. "It starts tomorrow."

Eventually, the sun goes down on another eventful day. As we look out the window, we can just see the ginger one next door's silhouette in the semi-darkness. He might be able to see Half-Sister in her undignified posture on the sofa. Regardless, all appears to be calm. What he is certainly unaware of is her forthcoming plan to accumulate good Karma, beginning tomorrow. Perhaps in this moment he is simply mourning the loss of one of his nine lives. I'm sure he has a few left. If Half-Sister were awake, she would surely comment on the fact that the ginger one next door, having leapt off the garden fence in the dark, has yet again managed to land on his feet.

The following day

The very next day there is an unexpected opportunity for Half-Sister to put her good intentions into practice. In the morning, Dad greets us as usual, and in his hand he has a dog lead. No surprise there. This normally means we are going for a walk, although on the odd occasion this is not the case. What happens next is our customary pre-walk ritual, as Half-Sister and I jostle for position. We must look like two spinning tops bouncing off the kitchen walls, only much noisier and not as graceful. This raucous behaviour has led to Dad refusing to take us for a walk together. At least he gets twice the exercise. Little did we know that today, all this is a rather pointless exercise, as it is Half-Sister who is going, regardless of my efforts. This is an interesting development and a slightly disturbing one for Half-Sister. Immediately after she realises it is her who is going she is bouncing down the steps and along the drive. Only she doesn't quite make it to the path, but instead ends up in the back seat of the car. Peering out the back window, Half-Sister can see the ginger one next door purveying his territory and eagerly watching the proceedings. If he knew where she was going, he might just fall of the wall and land on his head rather than his feet due to excess laughter. As the car pulls out the drive, Half-Sister's mind begins to calculate the options and to consider the issue of creating good Karma.

Option 1 – A nice walk in the countryside.

This is a possibility, but unlikely, as we don't usually take the car when we go for a walk. It has been known for us to go to the woods in the car, but this is a long shot, especially first thing in the morning and on a weekday. If by some miracle Half-Sister is going for a walk that requires a car journey, then good Karma can be gathered like falling leaves by walking nicely on the lead, coming back when called and not barking at other dogs. She is almost always friendly towards people, apart from strangers that knock on the door at night. When it comes to other dogs, however, boy does she dislike Jack Russells. When she was young, a Jack Russell tried to land one on Half-Sister. He missed, but since that day, like a Glasgow street-fighter, she always gets the first one in.

Option 2 – The vets.

This option is, without question, a strong contender, although Half-Sister has not been feeling dodgy of late. Visits to the vets usually happen when Half-Sister refuses her breakfast; this is the equivalent of Mum not wanting a glass of wine, or Dad turning the football off on the TV so he can watch Coronation Street. These are occurrences that are a great cause for concern, and would need medical intervention. Anyway, the car has turned off the road that leads to the vets and the woods for that matter, so option one and two are out the window. A confused and puzzled frown has emerged on Half-Sister's mush.

Option 3 – Holidays.

This is wishful thinking on Half-Sister's part and smacks of desperation. We have just been to the remote cottage in Scotland, there is no luggage, and we all go on holiday together.

Option 4 – Work.

We don't go to our Dad's place of work very often, but we have been before, so it's a possibility. It's nice, and the people are friendly. The last time we visited his office, we went for a walk because it's located in the countryside and right beside a nature reserve. The local pheasant population often pay a visit and look in the windows. We thought they were being curious to see who was inside, but it turns out they think it's another pheasant looking back at them. They get all wound up and excited and make a weird noise. It seems to us that pheasants are not the sharpest pencils in the box. Option 4 could well be the most likely destination, as they are definitely on the right road. Half-Sister's frown has receded and is replaced by a half smile. She is optimistic.

Reality – The groomers.

Now it's not the quality of the groomers that's in question here. After all, the lady who owns it actually won Crufts (well her dog did). It's also not the fear of looking like a springadoodle or a cockapoo when you come out either, because Mum always gives *strict* instructions on how she wants Half-Sister to be trimmed. Saying that, some of the dogs in there do have a hard time and come out decidedly dodgy-looking. As Dad says, if you cross a Shih Tzu with a poodle, you could get yourself into all kinds of trouble. Just to clarify things here, the groomers is definitely the destination, as the car has stopped right outside the door. The half smile has vanished as Half-Sister mutters under her breath. Bad Karma.

Her immediate reaction to this development is to turn to her favoured skill, honed over the years and perfect for such situations. Amazing as it might sound, Half-Sister can actually produce a convincing impersonation of a bag of cement. Dad turns into the builder's merchants (previously known as the groomers) and heads towards the front door. As Dad struggles with Half-Sister, she begins to reflect on our conversation about accruing good Karma. This has the effect of her shape-shifting into a bag of sand.

By the time they get inside the front door, Half-Sister has loosened the grip of reactive thoughts and transported herself from the DIY store to the groomers' reception. A nice young lady arrives to greet Dad; she is wearing a freshly-ironed uniform and is going to transform Half-Sister from a hairy Wookie to a sophisticated thing of beauty. She must be up for a challenge. The first thing that hits you when you walk into the reception is the smell - essence of poodle parlour. Half-Sister's nose begins to twitch, and traces of concrete begin to return to the legs. Dad hands her over to the young lady, who politely asks, 'The usual?' On this occasion, not necessarily, as she disappears into the building with Half-Sister in tow.

The groomer is doing her best to remain poised and in charge, but as the concrete impersonation returns with a vengeance, she looks more like a bricklayer's apprentice carrying their first load of bricks and wheeling a barrow at the same time. Half-Sister, still wearing her concrete overcoat, looks for possible escape routes. Now this, magical transformation is no quick fix. Half-Sister will be in there all morning, so there is plenty of time to practice mindfulness, kindness and compassion for all living beings. We hope.

Sometime later ......

Four hours later, Dad returns to the groomers to collect Half-Sister. After parting with his hard-earned cash, he watches the receptionist go off to collect the transformed one. Eventually she makes an appearance. If you didn't know better, you would think she was a different dog. Apart from the sleek appearance, every graceful movement is accompanied by a small cloud of talcum powder. She may look different, but we know it's her by the scowl on her face and the eagerness in the legs to get out of the door. Apparently, it took twenty-four breathing spaces and two loving kindness meditations to get through the ordeal. Plus whatever Half-Sister did.

Once she arrives back home, it is revealed in the debrief that Half-Sister was, indeed, very well-behaved. She practiced her breathing spaces, and showed appreciation for the groomer's hard work and the end result. It just goes to show that our thoughts are sometimes not how things unfold in reality, and that being kind *can* pay dividends. Looks like more good Karma in the bank. Half-Sister ends the debrief by sharing her wisdom for the day, which is becoming a daily ritual in this house.

> *I may not have gone where I intended to go, but I think I have ended up where I intended to be.*
> Douglas Adams

With that statement she turns on a sixpence and heads for the garden, leaving behind a vapour trail of talcum powder.

In the morning, I awake to thoughts circling in my mind about all this kindness and compassion stuff, and how being nice can get you a bag full of the right kind of Karma. After reflecting for a while, it seems to me that I may have been underestimating the merits of my Half-Sister. For starters, as I am the youngest, she has this habit of looking out for me; keeping an eye on me when I am in the garden, on a walk, or on holiday. She barks to tell me when grub's up, or a treat is imminent, and lets me have a drink first. Half-Sister even let me pinch her carrot once, although that was scary. I also get to have all the toys, and she puts up with me when I get carried away in the play fights (although if I go too far, the Half-Sister red mist rises and you have to run and hide). That's enough for now. I'm off to the garden for a game of catch, if I can bark anyone to come outside. Any more thoughts about the merits of Half-Sister and I'll be filling up. You can come over all emotional when you think nice thoughts.

Gratitude practice

The practice of gratitude has turned out to be a powerful practice, and in my case, very beneficial. There is scientific evidence that suggests taking time out to notice and reflect on things we are thankful for can actually create more positive emotions. This makes us feel more alive, compassionate, kind, have better sleep and a stronger immune system. This all has to be good, and might just mean fewer trips to the vet. We know all this because Google has a pal called Google Scholar; it's like Google but a bit of a swat. The fact is you can be grateful for anything if you make the effort - anything from a nice walk in the woods to a tiny bit of ginger snap that falls on the floor.

Today, Half-Sister and I have decided to play our new gratitude game. We made it up all by ourselves and are happy to share it. It involves being thankful for all the things in the day that turn out to be a nice experience. Half-Sister likes this game and gets very enthusiastic - she begins by shouting at the top of the stairs that she is grateful to have woken up and still be alive. It could be a long day.

By the time we get around to snoozing on the sofa all warm and cozy in the evening (something else we are grateful for), we have compiled a very comprehensive list of experiences that we are thankful and indebted to others for, and all this from one day. In fact, if it wasn't for all the kind and thoughtful things people do, we would be walking the streets or in the rescue centre. Now there's a thought. Talking about rescue centers and kind and compassionate acts, we remember the time Dad sponsored the springer spaniel rescue centre dog show. Trouble was, we weren't allowed to enter. Half-Sister reckons this is because Dad would have had to vote for us, otherwise what kind of message would he be giving out? Just in case he decides to sponsor the show again, Half-Sister is plotting a course of action. Her devious plan involves coinciding a trip to the groomers with the show dates. Not only will she look good, but Dad might not recognize her, or be blinded by the talcum powder clouds. Either way, it's a cunning plan. We will see if Half-Sister ever gets to activate the plan. In the meantime, it's back to the gratitudinal inquiry process, and the business of good Karma collection.

As the Buddha points out in his teachings, intention = action = consequences. We are making sure that our intentions are good and our actions are kind and compassionate, so that the consequences are tickety-boo (that's spaniel for agreeable). As night falls and we head for bed, we decide to stop for a moment and say a little prayer for all the creatures out in the cold. Half-Sister says it's okay to include all the cats, even the ginger one next door that is whining at the back door of his house to be let in. It is impossible to tell whether Half-Sister is having a compassionate moment here, or the ginger one next door is just keeping her awake. Not even the Buddha knows the answer to that one.

Words – it's complicated

It's been a while since we have heard anything from The Bookshelf on the issue of Karma, or anything else for that matter, but today he has sprung forth with words of wisdom. We have been spending a lot of time thinking about good and bad Karma, or in some cases evil Karma, but according to The Bookshelf there are more appropriate words than good or bad we could use. He tells us that from a Buddhist perspective we should perhaps substitute the words 'good and bad' with 'wholesome and unwholesome', or 'helpful and unhelpful'. Wholesome actions come from compassion, loving-kindness and wisdom. Unwholesome actions come from greed, hate and ignorance. Okey-dokey - we will not argue with the purveyor of all knowledge. It looks like I spoke to soon, because Half-Sister has decided to challenge The Bookshelf and declares that after that explanation, she is now well and truly confused about what word she should use and sums up The Bookshelf's talk as 'unhelpful'. The Bookshelf, attempting to use wit as a riposte, replies by suggesting that the fact that she has chosen 'unhelpful' rather than 'bad' or 'unwholesome' demonstrates that she is not confused. There now follows a period of silence that would do a Buddhist monastery proud. This is only interrupted by occasional grooming and random page-turning.

Later, and after careful consideration, it was agreed that we would use 'helpful and unhelpful' as the terms for our actions. It is approved because all that reference to wholesome and unwholesome had connotations around healthy and dodgy dog food. We didn't go with good and bad to keep The Bookshelf happy. Half-Sister pointed out that there are multiple ways of looking at all this stuff, and to clarify her argument, began to tell us the story of the great flood and the mouse.

The great flood and the mouse

The story begins when, after several days of torrential rain, Dad decided to take Half-Sister for a walk around the river. This was partly due to the fact she was going stir- crazy, having been stuck in the house for days, and also because the river, due to the inclement weather, was about to burst its banks and flood the street. Dad wanted to witness the spectacle as he had only read about previous floods in the local paper. As they crossed the bridge, you could see that the water had nearly reached the top. All the houses had sandbags at the front door and the locals were stationed along the river, discussing whether it would burst its banks or not. All very exciting for Dad and Half-Sister. Now there were all kinds of debris being carried at speed down the river, including trees, bikes and plastic pipes. Some of the debris had been washed up on the riverbank and the path, including a dead mouse. Before Dad could guide Half-Sister in the opposite direction it was gone, apart from its tail, which was hanging out of Half-Sister's mouth like the final piece of Mum's spaghetti bolognaise. Now Dad, being a resourceful soul, went for his bag of treats in his pocket faster than cowboys on the telly draw their guns, but it was all in vain. Down the hatch it went. Just for effect, Half-Sister recreates the gulp. We are stunned, slightly queasy, and could definitely have done without the action reply.

Now the point of this story, as far as Half-Sister is concerned, is this: was that a helpful or unhelpful action and what are the karmic consequences of the action? She has a theory about all this, and so explains the following. According to Half-Sister, the action was indeed helpful, and therefore no bad Karma will be coming her way. This is based on the fact that she did not intend to harm the mouse; it was already dead due to its inability to swim. In fact, through no fault of its own, the mouse was making the street untidy, and could have been declared a health hazard. She was actually doing the council a favour. As for the mouse, it was off for reincarnation, albeit by a slightly different route, but recycled all the same. You can't argue with that, so The Bookshelf and I didn't.

The river never did burst its banks, which was good news for all the people who live there, including our friend Wendy and her pack of spaniels. Thereafter followed a much-needed breathing space meditation to help us all deal with the trauma of the story.

Following this morning's 'Sermon on the Mount' declaration at the top of the stairs, Half-Sister continued later in the day by telling us that although lots of things have happened in the past, it is just that - the past. What's important now is what action we take in the present moment. With that final statement, she then heads for the sofa. After all that reflecting and considering, it's definitely time for a recovery snooze.

Puddle dodgers

Today it is raining, and it looks like one of those days where it will rain all day, just because it can and basically feels like it. It will also be the day when, as usual on these inclement occasions, I will be attacked by the mud, whereas Half-Sister will venture into all the same places and return without a speck. How does she do that? Everyone has gone to work so we have decided it's the ideal opportunity to have a study day in the dining room with The Bookshelf. He is happy to oblige, and thinks it sounds like a good idea as its raining cats and dogs out there. It should come as no surprise that Half-Sister begins the study day by asking The Bookshelf to explain the stupid comment about raining cats and dogs. If he looks out the window, he will see that it's not raining cats and dogs, or squirrels for that matter; it's only raining rain. After a brief shuffling of papers, he does his best to explain that it is simply an expression people use to describe that it's raining heavily. As that doesn't seem to pacify Half-Sister he comes up with another theory. A long, long time ago in old England, people used to have hay roofs, and the cats and dogs would sleep on the roof. When it rained, the roofs got slippery and the cats and dogs would slide off, hence the saying 'it's raining cats and dogs'. The Bookshelf seems confident with this explanation, and tells us it stems from Norse mythology. Half-Sister has that considering look on her face, and finally tells us that, in her opinion, it wouldn't need to be raining for the cats to fly off the roof. It would just need a springer spaniel and a robust ladder.

Before we further expand our minds with more newfound knowledge, we are going to explain the handy little practice called a *'breathing space'* we have been using. It's ideal for bringing mindfulness into daily life, even when it's not a rainy day, or for recovering from Half-Sister's graphic stories. You can just drop it into your day whenever you like. It's especially helpful if life is a bit low on the tickety-boo scale (in other words, when things get a bit difficult).

The breathing space (tickety-boo realignment)

Step 1 – Acknowledging

The practice begins by adopting the usual dignified posture; however, sometimes when you are out and about, you might just need to stop and do it in whatever posture you happen to be in. When you are settled, it's time to check in with whatever is going on, right now, in this moment. Noticing and acknowledging any experiences that are arising, even the difficult ones if you can. It's the mindfulness attitude of acceptance we are endeavouring to bring to this practice. Being with all our thoughts, emotions and physical sensations as they come and go, and allowing them to be just as they are.

Step 2 – Gathering

It's now time to move the attention to the breath. You can do this from wherever you can sense the breath entering and leaving the body. This could be the chest, abdomen or mouth. If you are a dog, it could be a big shiny black nose. Be with each breath from the very beginning to the very end, breathing in and breathing out. This helps to keep bringing us back to the present moment when we are distracted or hijacked by Wandering Mind.

Step 3 – Expanding awareness

Finally, we expand awareness around the breath to encompass the whole body, including the space it takes up, as if the whole body were breathing.

The whole sequence takes about three minutes, but

as we don't have watches in spaniel time, it takes as long as it takes.

After completing the practice, and with everything now realigned on the tickety-boo scale, it's over to The Bookshelf to continue the study session. Looking out the window, we can see that the garden is filling up with water. There is no sign of descending cats and dogs, but our next practice will definitely be mindful puddle-dodging.

Today's study day delivered by The Bookshelf has been most enlightening, and has deepened our knowledge and thoughts about Karma. In the morning, after researching the topic all night, The Bookshelf informs us of the following facts he thinks we need to take on board. The statement that got us thinking (bordering on over-pondering) is that, according to Buddhism, Karma is not some kind of criminal justice system in the sky. It's not all about getting rewarded or punished for your actions. It's more like a natural law, and here is the big one - Karma begins at once. Once set in motion, Karma tends to spread in many directions, like the ripples on a pond or in today's case, like giant puddles in a soggy garden. In other words, what you do now impacts on your life right now. The Bookshelf has also informed us that Karma is not mysterious or hidden, and that once we get our heads around it we will be able to observe it everywhere. Just then, as if pre-arranged, our little friend the robin arrives in the garden for a bath in one of the many puddles. He is having a whale of a time, when suddenly the ginger one next door, who was chasing birds all day yesterday, launches himself off the garden fence. The robin is well-aware of the ginger one, and manoeuvres away to the safety of the sky. To the great delight of Half-Sister, the ginger one next door does a giant belly flop in the puddle. He then skids through numerous other puddles before coming to a halt, *very* wet, and *very* muddy. Half-Sister, who was chasing the ginger one next door all day yesterday, is laughing so hard she bangs her head on the table. The Bookshelf looks at me, I look at him and together, we both look at the ginger one next door and Half-Sister. All that is required is a nod of understanding.

Later in the day the laughter subsides, and the bump on Half-Sister's head begins to recede. The ginger one next door, after much preening, is back to his ginger best and is once more positioned on the garden fence. All is as it should be, and so we begin the serious business of accumulating good Karma through skilful action. Every moment is an opportunity to shape our future. Like the following quote says, this is a chance not to be missed:

Karma is the law of cause and effect – an unbreakable law of the cosmos. Your actions create your future. The reason your fate is never sealed is because you have free will. Therefore, your future cannot already be written. That would not be fair. Life gives you chances. This is one of them.
Tree of Awakening

Upon reflection under the bamboo

Eventually, the rain decides to stop and it's time for reflection to begin under the bamboo. In timely fashion, the occasional drip acts as a reminder to concentrate on the present moment. We are thankful for the efforts of The Bookshelf for all his input, especially the bit about Karma starting in this life. That got us thinking and laughing. All this talk about action and consequences has focused our minds, and we are doing our best to make each moment a nice moment. When other people or beings do nasty stuff, we are learning to let it go and to walk away. We will trust in our new friend Karma to sort it out - all we have to do is wait. In the meantime, Half-Sister thinks the constant dripping of rain on her head is payback for all the plants she has dug up in the garden. Not forgetting the plants she ate that made her icky-sicky. That was instant Karma. To end this reflective period on Karma, we decide a sound meditation would be appropriate, so settling in, we both tune in to the sounds emanating from nature. We can hear the wind in the trees, the birds, and the sound of an occasional drip landing on Half-Sister's head. If we concentrate really hard we can just hear in the background the distant sound of a ginger chuckle, much to Half-Sister's annoyance.

8
Loving kindness – befriending next door's cat

> *I think dogs are the most amazing creatures; they give unconditional love. For me, they are the role models for being alive.*
>
> Gilda Radner

The nearest comparison would be a death ray in a sci-fi movie.

WE HAVE UNCOVERED THROUGH our research a meditation that we feel might just help Half-Sister comply with the precept of non-harming and not killing things. She is currently having immense difficulty in sticking to this precept, as every time she sees next door's cat (or any cat for that matter), she wanders straight off the *Eightfold Path* and down the road to the village of bad Karma. In the blink of an eye, Right Intention becomes wrong intention, and Right Action switches to wrong action. There is plenty of effort and concentration, but definitely not in the way the Buddha meant. Matters have not been helped by the startling discovery that before we arrived in this house, two cats resided here. This has done nothing for Half-Sister's frame of mind. She has now taken to watching Mum clean the house, has read the vacuum cleaner manual twice and has studied all the cleaning material instructions and contents. As this is bordering on OCD (Obsessive Cat Disorder), decisive action is needed before we resort to calling BUPA (Borderline Unusual Pet Activity). We are therefore hoping that the introduction of a *'loving kindness meditation'* will help Half-Sister come to terms with this shocking discovery, and get her back on track with the Eightfold Path. The original name for this practice is *Metta Bhavana*. Metta means love (not in a slushy way, mind), and Bhavana is development, or cultivation; hence 'loving kindness'. We are thinking that if we ever get another spaniel in this house, we should call it Metta. Its Buddhist name would be Right Cuddly!

First of all we need to familiarise ourselves with how

you do the practice. The instructions kindly supplied by The Bookshelf inform us that the meditation includes the use of words, images, and feelings to bring about loving kindness and friendliness towards others and ourselves. Each time we recite the phrases, we are planting an intention of loving wishes over and over in our hearts. As usual, we have to find a quiet spot and then sit for about twenty minutes. This time it's being with the breath and reciting inwardly the following phrases:

May I be filled with loving kindness.
May I be safe from inner and outer dangers.
May I be well in body and mind.
May I be at ease and happy.

The structure of the practice is to begin by wishing loving kindness towards yourself. Let's face it, if you can't wish yourself loving kindness, you have got very little chance of doing it for others. As you repeat the words, you picture yourself in your mind's eye, just how you are right now, and hold the image in a heart full of loving kindness. Repeat the above phrases over and over and allow them to permeate into the body and mind, as the sense of loving kindness begins to grow. When you have established loving kindness towards yourself, you can then move on to someone else, thereby expanding the meditation towards others. We could choose Mum or Dad for this next step, or each other, or our friend Wendy who lives down by the river. She has got three spaniels, so could definitely use the input. She has a cocker spaniel, a springer spaniel, and one that's a combination of the two - a sprocker. They used to be called mongrels, but now they have trendy names like cockapoo, springadoodle, or cockadoodledoo. Perhaps we should choose the sprocker, as it might help with her identity crisis. Anyway, picturing the other person/dog and then repeating the phrases:

May you be filled with loving kindness.
May you be safe from inner and outer dangers.
May you be well in body and mind.
May you be at ease and happy.

Obviously, all the potential choices so far have been people we like, or friendly mutts from down the street. It is recommended that after a while we try to expand the practice to those we are not so keen on. That's a tricky one, as it would include certain vets, horses, people that knock on the door unannounced, small dogs like a Jack Russell, groups of small children (especially on scooters), the garden hose and of course, CATS.

We have decided that it might be best if Half-Sister builds up to wishing next door's cat loving kindness. As far as this practice is concerned, we have plumped for the vet. After all, she does look after us. There was some discussion regarding people that knock on the door unannounced because it's Halloween soon (whatever that's all about). Half-Sister liked the idea of a 'loving spookiness meditation,', but decided better of it. Last year there were *loads* of them at the door, all shapes and sizes, all suitably horrible and drooling for treats. There was even a dog dressed as a skeleton! Sometime in the future we will have to include him in our loving kindness mediations, because he wouldn't have donned that outfit willingly. He didn't scare anybody but himself that night.

The final option in the meditation is to offer loving kindness to all beings - everything on the planet. Technically this would include the ginger one next door, but as we don't have to say his name, Half-Sister has agreed. It's a start.

May they be filled with loving kindness.
May they be safe from inner and outer dangers.
May they be well in body and mind.
May they be at ease and happy.

As we have now sorted ourselves, the vet and everyone else on the planet, it's time for a well-earned rest. This is followed by a trip around the garden and some tennis ball aerobics.

Reflecting on the loving kindness meditation, we have decided that it has great promise, and will practice it every day in the hope that Half-Sister discovers her feline side. As it is Halloween coming up, we are practicing our barking and looking fierce faces. A little bit of us is also hoping that the West Highland terrier from down the street does not turn up dressed as a skeleton again. Half-Sister says he will be scarred for life, but is consoling herself by imagining the ginger one next door dressed as a toilet brush. There is a *lot* of loving kindness to practise.

Fence meditation

Today, much to our surprise, Half-Sister has taken matters into her own hands and made an appointment with The Bookshelf to explore the problematic issue of cats, and why she can't resist chasing them. The thinking behind this move is that to change something, you first have to understand the rationale behind the problem. Although Half-Sister has never thought of it as a problem before. The Bookshelf has a book in his repertoire called "The History of Dogs,' which seems a good place to start. The first thing that arises in this search for answers is: 'Why do dogs chase cats?' Well, approximately twelve-thousand years ago, dogs were domesticated by human beings. Well, that's what they think. Prior to that, it stands to reason they must have been wild animals. Taking all that into consideration, chasing a cat is therefore just a natural behaviour. Back then we would have been scavengers, so a cat is simply food (along with anything else we can find). This is why most dogs will eat anything. This hunting behaviour is hard-wired in our brains, and is called 'prey drive,' so when we see something to chase, we are off, even if we have just had our dinner. Let's hope our meditation practice can help us to rewire our brains and be more compassionate. No wonder the ginger one next door legs it at the speed of light - as far as Half-Sister is concerned, he is just one big ginger biscuit. As for being classed as a scavenger, I think I can relate to that one, as Half-Sister has eaten most things over the years. A lot of her munching escapades have been entered into spaniel folklore in this house. The stories always do the rounds at Christmas, or when we have visitors, and never cease to amaze the listener. It would fill a book on its own if we went into detail, but the most famous incident is eating all the tinsel off the Christmas tree and then producing gift-wrapped poo the following day. Other items that have disappeared over the years include tin foil, Raggy the rope toy, plants, soil, material from Mum's sewing project, a mouse, and her all-time favourite, paper hankies. So I think it's safe to say Half-Sister in a scavenger with a capital S. After a productive session with The Bookshelf, Half-Sister seems to have it set in her mind why she chases and dislikes cats. The question now is, will she actually do anything about it?

The following day, Half-Sister gathers all her *loving kindness* and *beginner's mind* and astonishes us all by heading to the garden with the sole purpose of meditating through the fence whilst looking at the ginger one next door. If Half-Sister were a car, she would be shifting from 'prey drive' to neutral. Unfortunately, as no driving test has been passed and only the theory in place, it could be a bumpy ride. Now, it is important to say at this point that Half-Sister staring through the gaps in the fence at the ginger one next door is not in itself unusual. In fact, it's a daily occurrence, along with pacing up and down and the barking ritual. However, meditating with *loving kindness* with the ginger one in attendance is the equivalent of the Titanic floating up the river saying it has just been hiding all along.

To begin this monumental moment in meditation

history, Half-Sister sets herself in an upright, dignified posture, takes a few mindful breaths and then plants her gaze through the gaps in the fence and straight at the ginger one next door's eyeballs. It's classic. The nearest comparison would be a death ray in a sci-fi movie. The ginger one is statuesque, and very, very confused. In comparison, the ginger one next door has definitely not adopted a dignified posture. His posture is more like that of a lookout at a bank robbery - on high alert, checking everything, and prepared to raise the alarm at any moment. Half-Sister begins by bringing *Beginner's Mind* to the practice and noticing the ginger one as if she had never ever seen him before. It has to be said that he is incredibly ginger - even his eyeballs are ginger. It's as if he had seriously overdone the Irn Bru the night before. His coat is actually stripy when you get up close and he has a big, bushy tail. Surprisingly, he looks much smaller than you'd imagine when you get a good look at him. Maybe it's the safety of being behind the fence, or simply fear that is keeping the ginger one rooted to the spot. Seeing that so far all is going well, Half-Sister cracks on. She starts the proceedings by wishing herself *loving kindness*. After all, she needs all the help she can get because the desire to splat the ginger one is monumental; the self-control is impressive so far.

After grounding herself for a while, Half-Sister then moves on to the awkward bit. Albeit through gritted teeth, she wishes the ginger one next door the following:

May he be filled with loving kindness.
May he be safe from inner and outer dangers.
May he be well in his stripy ginger body and mind.
May he be at ease and happy.

She repeats the lines several times whilst holding the death ray gaze through the garden fence. Miraculously, it's still holding firm as the ginger one remains motionless and transfixed. Now, I don't think he is filled with loving kindness yet, or feels safe from inner and outer dangers. He may feel well in his stripy body and moggy-like mind, but he *definitely* feels at ease and happy when Half-Sister ends the practice and heads for the kitchen. I'm sure I see a hint of a tear in his eye. On the other hand that might just be relief. Half-Sister has gone for a lie down; she is pleased with her progress, but is praying that none of the local spaniels witnessed the event.

The following day, just as the afternoon sun is setting on the garden, he is back, stripy body and all. He seems a little less agitated this time, and has perhaps moved from a bank robber lookout to a stake-out cop. Saying that, his tail is swishing back and forth, which is always a sign of slight unease. Half-Sister spies him through the window and quotes a line from her favourite movie Home Alone: "So, are you hungry for more?" She saunters into the garden, casting a spaniel shadow as she goes. The Bookshelf, who is totally gobsmacked by this development, is frantically searching for a book on hypnosis, as this is the only explanation he has come up with.

Half-Sister has now arrived at the fence and is easing herself into a dignified posture in preparation for another round of the *loving kindness* meditation. This is how it continues, day in day out, the ginger one next door would turn up bang on time, and every day, Half-Sister obliging by reciting the *loving kindness* practice. Sometimes he purrs, and other times he stays silent, transfixed by Half-Sister, the moggy meditation teacher.

After several weeks, Half-sister's reputation is enhanced by the arrival of participant number two - the white one two doors along. Well, the almost - white one, all apart from his tail, which has a black tip. Maybe he was all-over black in a previous life, and has been reincarnated with a dodgy re-spray. By this time, The Bookshelf has resigned himself to just watching through the window in amazement. Books on hypnosis, group hypnosis, telepathy, tracker beams and death rays have all produced zilch.

By the end of the month, Half-Sister's moggy meditation group had expanded to five. This included the ginger one next door, the white one two doors along, the two fat ones across the street and the oriental one. The oriental one is the new kid on the block. The Bookshelf reckons he comes from foreign parts. He has scary blue eyes, and sneaks along the curb like a snake that has swallowed a brick. We are not sure about him yet. The fat ones, however, are definitely in need of some *loving kindness,* as they are a bit under-the-weather at the moment. The vet has got them on steroids for their asthma and they are pumped-up like four-legged sumo wrestlers. You can hear them wheezing miles away; even Half-Sister has given up chasing them in case they burst. Anyway, they are all lined up in their various dignified postures, awaiting the Zen master spaniel to begin. Hopefully this is it, otherwise we will need a bigger fence.

After spending some time on posture, Half-Sister then moves on to the breath. This is all good apart from the fat ones; however, they are doing their best, wheezing in, wheezing out. Half-Sister works her way through all the verses, and then it's a wrap.

Due to the increasing demands on her time, Half-Sister has allocated Mondays as 'Loving Kindness Meditation Day'. It's the usual five suspects each week, plus the occasional stray that turns up. She sometimes fits in an extra session if the fat ones (or anyone else for that matter) are due at the vets. This is usually a breathing space for times of difficulty. As for chasing them, well, that would be bad for business, wouldn't it?

Upon reflection under the bamboo

Apart from the transformative effect on Half-Sister's relationship with cats and her new found desire to be a meditation teacher, we are wondering how all this loving kindness practice might be impacting on the lives of the moggies in Half-Sister's meditation class. We have noticed that there appears to be less in-street fighting and more sitting on the fence admiring the trees and the sky, although it's hard to tell as they also do that when they are hunting. It would be nice to think they are pondering life, rather than ending it. To stop complacency setting in, and to protect her reputation, Half-Sister will occasionally bat them off the fence. Just like a Zen meditation teacher whacks their students with a stick to stop them from falling asleep during meditation practice. It would be a great result if Half-Sister has started a circle of compassion, and that all beings are benefitting from the loving kindness practice she is teaching. The Buddha would surely smile at that. As for The Bookshelf, well, he has realised that some things in life are just mysteries of the Universe, and go beyond the pages of time and perceived wisdom. His words, not ours.

9
Playing in the Field of Awareness

There are moments of existence when time and space are more profound, and the awareness of existence is immensely heightened.
Charles Baudelaire

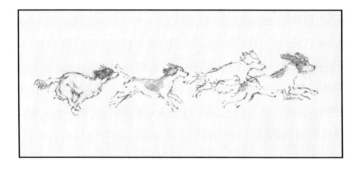

Today, the so called Field of Awareness is far from empty. We have visitors, and Half-Sister is excited.

THUS FAR WE HAVE been practising focusing our attention on just one thing at a time, like the breath, the body or sounds. After consulting several books on the subject, the general opinion seems to be that this is called *Mindful, Focused Awareness*. If we practise our meditation on a regular basis, we may uncover the opportunity to make our mind concentrated and still. That said, we have recently discovered that there is actually another kind of awareness called *Mindful, Open Awareness*. This is described as a more relaxed awareness - wider, and taking in everything. Half-Sister thinks this might be similar to when, in meditation, we are watching the flow of our experiences arising and passing. We can be mindful of something in particular, but also aware of everything in the background at the same time. This appears similar to the last part of the sitting meditation, when we are encouraged to watch all our experiences come and go. There has been a lot of reference in our studies about expanding something called the Field of Awareness. Fortunately for us, Half-Sister knows exactly where this field is and how to get to it, so we are off.

With Half-Sister leading the way, we head out the front door and down the road. On the way we pass the human vets; as usual, it's busy and there is a queue. We stay low and pretend we don't notice. It could be vaccination day. It's then time to cross the road and head straight down towards the leafy path. Now, walking down the road is not as straight forward as that last sentence sounds. It normally takes a while, as Half-Sister insists on doing her impression of a car mechanic. All the way down the street, every car has to be inspected, including its tyres, exhaust system and brakes, before she passes it and issues an MOT (Minus Old Tomcats). The funny thing is, the only time an old tomcat was discovered under a car was when I was passing by, just minding my own business. I still have the scar on the end of my nose to prove it.

In autumn, the leafy path comes into its own. It's like a soft carpet underfoot, and there are so many colours and smells. When descending the path it's best to stay in the middle - if you wander to either side, you get attacked by the spiky burrs. They are determined little fellows, and insist on coming home with you. Half-Sister says they can get into places you didn't even know you had. Interestingly, it's referred to as the leafy path all year round, even when it's lost its leafiness. Part of the path has steps - twenty to be exact. We know this as Dad and I counted them on the way up one day, and on the way down to make sure. It's on the way down, despite the existence of a handrail, that the combination of leaves, steps and spaniels can combine to cause mayhem. When this happens, the leafy path has A & E written all over it.

This was no more evident than when Mum decided to take Half-Sister down the leafy path on a winter's afternoon: the sun may have been shining, but the ice lay in wait, like a cat stalking a mouse. Just as she got to the bottom of the steps, whoosh! Unable to stand, never mind walk, there was no alternative but to call the mobile human vets. Now Half-Sister was very young when this happened, so she just sat there looking all puppy-like while they waited for the ambulance to arrive. A nice lady who had witnessed the whole event kindly offered to take Half-Sister to her house, which was just around the corner, until Dad could come and collect her. What happened at that lady's house remains a mystery to this day. Dad's version of the story is that the lady looked very frazzled, when he got there and gave the impression that she was very relieved to see him. There was newspaper and bits of cardboard ripped up and strewn all over the kitchen floor. She told Dad that she had a cat, and that Half-Sister had chased it up the stairs and then returned to eat the cat's dinner. She relayed all this to Dad with a smile on her face; however, her shaking hands and twitching may have given away her true feelings regarding the Half-Sister experience. Eventually, (after a further inspection of the house) Half-Sister skidded down the stairs accompanied by a lump of cat food positioned delicately on her nose. There was no sign of the cat. Dad reckons that Half-Sister had an evil grin on her face that he had not seen before. However, we have all seen that evil grin appear on many occasions since that fateful day. As they finally left the lady's house, she told Dad that, although she was a cat person, if she ever had a dog she would like one just like Half-Sister. All we can surmise from that statement is that she had either just come out of hospital, is a politician, or was still in shock. Anyway, we digress from the leafy path and the journey to the Field of Awareness.

Eventually, when you arrive at the bottom of the leafy path (whether that happens to be standing up or on your bum), you can see the entrance to what Half-Sister is referring to as the Field of Awareness. Sometimes the field is completely empty apart from grass and trees; the occasional bird might appear, or the odd hopping rabbit, but that's about it. Trees and bushes surround the field and on one side, the trees hide the river. You can also get to the field via the little bridge that spans the river. This is the same river that Half-Sister's dead mouse journeyed to reincarnation. The bridge is green and has spaces in-between the slats where you can see the water flowing by. It is also narrow and not really big enough for two dogs and their owners to pass, so sometimes you have to wait your turn. The river holds many memories for Half-Sister, including the day when she was a puppy and Mum threw a stick in the river. Without thinking, Half-Sister jumped in after it. She did eventually make it back to the riverbank, but was far from impressed with the experience. That was her first introduction to water and coughing and spluttering. It could also be the reason she hates the bath so much.

Today, the so called Field of Awareness is far from empty. We have visitors, and Half-Sister is excited. Wendy, who lives down by the river, is already in the field and has brought her three spaniels. Using my limited grasp of mathematics, I reckon three plus two makes five spaniels, which seems far too many for the golden retriever standing at the entrance by the river. His owner might be considering venturing into the field, but the dog looks as if he would willingly go to the vets rather than enter Spanialmania.

So, a quick inventory: a liver/white springer spaniel, a black cocker spaniel and a black/white combination of the two (sprocker), plus yours truly (black/white) and Half-Sister (liver/white). Now at this point I should mention that the black cocker spaniel, after a sad mishap, has only one eye. Apart from this, he is fine. He may have limited vision, but as he is the oldest he may have seen it all before anyway. For this reason we have anointed him with his Buddhist name, which is Right Side Only.

As soon as we enter the field, we are let off our leads and the exploration begins. You might compare this to letting go of the breath in meditation and just seeing what arises and passes, being with our experiences as they come and go. The coming and going of so many spaniels has eventually led to the golden retriever persuading his owner to take him someplace else. Anywhere else. Playing in the field has got me thinking about life and meditation. It seems to me that running in the field is just one long practice - one long series of moments. Sometimes I am noticing the breath; other times it's the sensations from running and chasing. Added to this is the experience of listening to sounds, especially barking and growling. One thing I am not doing is remembering the last time I did this, or wondering when the next time will be. I am just running in the moment. I'll leave the other stuff to the humans.

While I have been enjoying myself running in circles with the spaniel pack, Half-Sister has been working on creating some good Karma. Perhaps this has emanated from all the *loving kindness* practice she has done recently.

The first action on the road-to-good-Karma collection involves Half-Sister cheering up the one-eyed cocker spaniel. She does this by telling him that he is not missing anything to the left, because all the good stuff is actually on the right. He seems to like that. Next up is an in-depth conversation with the sprocker about the benefits of being both a cocker and a springer spaniel. Half-Sister suggests that you can be a cocker one day and a springer the next day, depending on what you fancy on the day. If you can't be bothered to choose be a sprocker, just be yourself. This has cheered the sprocker up no end, and the identity crisis seems to be over. Half-Sister seems pleased with her herself, and has a spring in her step as she returns to running around and sniffing with the pack. After half an hour of charging around the so-called Field of Awareness, it's time to head back up the leafy path towards home. Just as we are almost at the front door of our house, Half-Sister suddenly spies the post lady doing her rounds. Now, Half-Sister and the post lady go back a long way. When she was a puppy, she helped deliver all the letters on our estate and was rewarded with one of the post lady's special biscuits. 'Helped' might not be the word the post lady would use, and the biscuit might have been to distract Half-Sister and save the soggy letters, but Half-Sister was on a mission that day. These biscuits are kept in the post lady's pocket in case she encounters an unruly mutt, or in this case, a trainee springer spaniel post-dog. It is this memory stored in Half-Sister's mind that results in all her accumulated good Karma disappearing as fast as a squirrel up a tree. The truth is that the post lady, like most of Half-Sister's victims, isn't even aware that she has been mugged. Half-Sister can take a paper hanky or a biscuit out of your pocket and you'd have no idea it had gone until it was too late. Today, this was the post lady's fate. In a flash, her store of emergency biscuits had vanished. To be honest, it's a skill to behold; however, when we get inside the house, Half-Sister heads straight for the garden and positions herself under the bamboo, stepping over the ants as she goes. By the look on her face she is definitely pondering her misdemeanour, and is to be avoided at all costs. The Bookshelf can see Half-Sister from the window and thinks she is being too hard on herself. He has revisited the Buddha's teachings and has some words of wisdom that I have to relay to her.

The Buddha reaffirmed on many occasions that his teachings are a training pathway - they are guidelines for an ethical life. They are not rules, and we can all learn from our mistakes. Half-Sister tells us that it's the precept of 'not taking what was not given' that she has broken. She realises now that if she had been patient and wise, she would probably have been given a biscuit anyway.

With a wise and cheeky grin Half-Sister trots off to stare at the ginger one next door. Balance is restored once again. After a while, she returns to the house and joins The Bookshelf and I, who are having a discussion about awareness. We are not getting very far in our analysis, so are happy to see her, as she has a habit of changing the subject. Several moments later, Half-Sister unleashes another one of her pearls of wisdom. I will do my best to translate.

According to Half-Sister we cannot be our bodies because the body doesn't do what you tell it - it does its own thing. If you have an iffy tummy, you cannot just tell the body to pack it in, because it doesn't listen. Then there is the mind. When you are doing your best to concentrate on the breath and that little pest Wandering Mind does a runner, who is it that collects her? It's not the mind, because the mind can't collect itself. To summarise that little lot, we are not our bodies and we are not our minds. For that reason, we must be awareness. And with that, she heads for the kitchen.

The Bookshelf and I have no answer to all that and so we resign ourselves to pondering, but soon give in. From the kitchen, Half-Sister informs us that awareness wants it's dinner. Later that evening, around the time we have our evening snooze on the sofa, the final sentence of the day arrives from Half-Sister: "Awareness is like a flashlight which pierces the veil of illusion and illuminates what is hidden behind it." After, that we close our eyes and slip into the land of non-awareness, only slightly disturbed by The Bookshelf frantically turning pages in the dining room.

The Buddha under the bamboo

The following morning, who should turn up under the bamboo but the Buddha himself! Now, he hadn't trekked all the way from India just to see us, but merely arrived from the garden centre down the road. Still, it was a nice touch from Dad to go and get him, and to position him in our favourite place. He certainly looks very regal, serene and peaceful, and we like him, even though he is taking up most of the space under the bamboo. Half-Sister is the most excited she has been since the day she went to the beach for the first time. After sitting next to him for a while, she finally proclaims that we can now reflect under the bamboo with the boss-man. He has a half-smile on his face which Half-Sister is putting down to the fact that he has now been reunited with his dog Right Nuisance after all these years. Just to impress him even further, she proceeds to demonstrate the sit, down and twirl tricks she learnt at puppy class. Half-sister is definitely taking no chances here. As evening arrives, so does the rain and the wind. The rain is lashing through the bamboo and the wind is so strong it's bending the top branches until they are almost touching the ground. All this is resulting in the Buddha getting extremely wet. Half-Sister, who is watching intently through the window, simply proclaims, "Sitting like a mountain, unmoved, he's not bothered by the weather - he's not bothered by anything."

At the next moggy meditation class, Half-Sister instructs them all to take note of how the Buddha is sitting under the bamboo - a perfect example of a dignified posture. Eagerly, they all shuffle into position as they attempt to imitate the Buddha, much to Half-Sister's approval. It's like the master and his apprentice - they are keen to please. It is, however, slightly unnerving when they all try to replicate the Buddha's half smile. It's difficult to describe. The words that come to mind are 'purry grimace', or in the case of the asthmatic fat ones, a steroid-induced wheezy smirk. As they are all peering through the garden fence, The Bookshelf decides to read a book to take his mind off the gruesome sight. He says it reminds him of a horror story he once read, but scarier. When they have all settled into a dignified grinning posture, Half-Sister begins the meditation class.

Sitting like a mountain (not bothered meditation)

Inspired by the Buddha's attitude as he sat under the bamboo in the inclement weather, The Bookshelf kindly searched and found Half-Sister a *Mountain Meditation* recording. In honour of the Buddha's arrival, we are all going to give it a go. Plus, Half-Sister would like to practise it with a view to trying it out on the moggy meditation group next week. As it's raining cats and dogs outside, we have decided to practise indoors today. As far as the weather is concerned, we are currently still bothered but are practising towards being not bothered.

The Mountain Meditation is usually done in a sitting position - for us, that's once again on our bums; for humans, it's usually in a straight-backed chair. To start the practice we have to get a sense of any sensations created by sitting, paying attention to contact. Then we are instructed to find a position of stability and poise, a bit like the dogs at Crufts on the telly. After a short while, we are ready to close our eyes and tune in to the breath. The voice on the recording kindly reminds us that it's the sensations of breathing we are paying attention to, rather than thinking about the breath. Very helpful. We are to allow the body to be still and sit with a sense of dignity, just like the Buddha in the garden. The next instruction is a little confusing, as it instructs us to take a long pause before continuing. As ours are quite short, we will just crack on regardless.

Now, as we sit in our dignified posture, we are to imagine in our mind's eye a beautiful mountain. It can be one we have visited, or we can just make it up. We are not sure if we have ever visited a mountain, although we have seen some pretty big hills in our time, such as in the Lake District, The Cheviots, and in Scotland when on holiday. I have decided to plump for a big hill like the one I saw in Scotland; however, Half-Sister has gone for a giant mountain in the Himalayas. She apparently tuned into Planet Earth one day after stealing the TV remote, and Sir David Attenborough told her all about it. We are encouraged to look at our mountain/hill any way we like - from afar or close up. We can even imagine that we are actually standing on it, as long as we notice how solid and unmoving it is.

We are to notice and explore whether there is any snow, trees, flowers or animals on our chosen lump of earth. My big hill has snow at the top, and Half-Sister's mountain is covered in snow. There are probably rabbits about too, but we are pretending there are none to avoid unnecessary distraction. Like any meditation, there is always the potential for a visit from Wandering Mind. Anything can trigger an appearance and, in this case, it was the word snow. Immediately upon hearing the word, she is recalling the time it snowed and everybody got snowed in on the estate. Nobody could get to work, the kids couldn't get to school, and so the only thing worth doing was making snowmen. Now, for a while, all was well. Half-Sister was in the front garden with Dad and was on her best behaviour. This blissful scene all changed in the blink of an eye when someone down the street, in their wisdom, decided that their snowman should have a carrot nose. Bad move. The rest of the tale is written in Half-Sister folklore. In the time it takes to spin in a circle, Half-Sister had covered a hundred yards, flown through the air, demolished the snowman and returned with the carrot. She left behind *total* devastation. The parents were confused, children were crying their eyes out, and the snowman was no longer a man - just snow. It was left to Dad to pacify everyone and give out free carrots. Goodness knows what bad Karma was accumulated on that day.

   After that short interlude instigated by Wandering Mind, our attention is now back and so on we go with the meditation. After observing the mountain for a while, we then move on to the next section, which is to imagine that we can bring the mountain into our body so we *become* the mountain. Grounded in our sitting posture, our head becomes the lofty peak and our body becomes the mass of the mountain, solid and unmoving. With each breath we become a little bit more like a giant breathing mountain (or a big hill in my case), still, centred, grounded and unmoving. I am doing my best here; however, Half-Sister has called upon her bag of cement impersonation after a visit to the Himalayan branch of the DIY shop. She is, as solid as a rock, and is therefore going nowhere.

As we sit, it's time to bring awareness to the fact that the sun is travelling across the sky, (in our mind's eye that is). Constantly changing, but always just being itself. Shadows and colours are changing moment-by-moment. There are streams, melting snow, waterfalls, plants and wildlife. Blimey, there is a lot going on! As we sit with our mountain and big hill impersonations, we are guided to see and feel how night follows day, and day follows night. Warming sun followed by cool night-sky, stars, and then the dawning of a new day. Through all this activity, the mountain/hill (and us) just sits, experiencing the change in each moment, yet always being itself. It remains still as the seasons flow into one another, and the weather changes moment-by-moment. Half-Sister, who has not budged an inch since the start of the practice, has expressed concern about the fact that we have been practising through several nights and days. Not to mention through a range of pleasant and inclement weather, and all the seasons of the year. All this without a sniff of a drink, dinner, or even a treat! Plus, she is getting older by the minute, and her fur doesn't know whether to stay or go. Never mind - she will stay with it, as the Buddha is watching from the garden. Un-relentlessly the voice on the recording ploughs on, and unwaveringly we stay seated like a mountain and a big hill, albeit hungry ones. In any season, we may find ourselves enshrouded by clouds or fog or pelted by freezing rain. A shiver works its way down Half-Sister's body and ends with the shake of her tail. None of this matters to the mountain/hill, which at all times is essentially itself.

In the same way that we can sit in meditation and experience being as grounded as a mountain or a big hill, so we can embody the same stillness in the face of everything that changes in our own lives. We experience constantly the changing nature of our mind and body, the outer world, light and dark, activity and inactivity. Talking of activity, we have just been paid a visit by Wandering Mind, who is wearing a bright-yellow anorak with matching hat and wellies. She doesn't stay long, as she informs us she is busy making a fire.

It may help to see that our thoughts, feelings, preoccupations, emotions and the things that we experience are very much like the weather on the mountain. The weather in our own lives is not to be ignored, but encountered and known for what it is - held in awareness. Mountains and hills have this to teach us if we let them in. So Half-Sister and I sit like mountains for the remaining time until we hear the bells that signify the end of the practice. Whilst somewhere in the far reaches of our minds, smoke is gently rising.

Upon reflection under the bamboo

It somehow miraculously unfolded that Half-Sister knew more about awareness than she thought. Where this wisdom comes from is a mystery. She even used the Field of Awareness as a metaphor, and we are still not sure what a metaphor is. She may have half-inched a biscuit from the post lady's pocket when she wasn't looking, but even *that* was turned into a lesson. All the Loving Kindness towards others in the field was impressive and must have surely gained Half-Sister some good Karma. We are now sitting either side of our new friend the Buddha for this reflection, and are pleased to report that he has dried out from the stormy weather (not that he was ever bothered). The sun is shining and we have had our dinner. This has all aided our recovery from the Himalayan trek and the big hill expedition. We are pleased to report that the fire is out. I am beginning to look at my Half-Sister in a new light and starting to wonder if she actually *is* related to Right Nuisance after all. Certainly the arrival of the Buddha in the garden has elevated her meditation practice and her study with The Bookshelf. Today she even told me that cats were sentient beings that just needed pointing in the right direction. I am not sure whether that last statement is the arising of wisdom or a prerequisite to a vet's appointment.

10

The Dharma, Dogma, and the Ultimate Truth

Your time is limited, so don't waste it living someone else's life. Don't be trapped by dogma — which is living with the results of other people's thinking. Don't let the noise of other's opinions drown out your own inner voice. And most important, have the courage to follow your heart and intuition. They somehow already know what you truly want to become. Everything else is secondary.

Steve Jobs

As the light fades, Half-Sister can be seen outside in the garden staring into a puddle.

BEFORE WE GET INTO the serious business of exploring what the *Dharma, Dogma* and *The Ultimate Truth* actually is, we would just like to say on a less serious note that we think Dharma and Dogma would make wicked names for two springer spaniels. While we are on the subject of excellent names for dogs, we also like Karma, but you would need to be careful it didn't come back and bite you on the bum. The quote from Steve Jobs at the top of the page is one of our Dad's favourites, so there you go Dad.

The opening contribution comes from The Bookshelf, who tells us that Dharma is held lightly, whilst Dogma is held tightly. He is in a very poetic mood today. What is the Dharma? Well if you Google it you get "Cosmic law and order." We are not sure about this explanation. Even if it is true, it sounds like the meditation police will come and arrest you if you let your practice slip. We much prefer that the teachings of the Buddha are often referred to as the 'Dharma'. Seemingly, the word Dharma is closely associated with 'truth' - a truth that you have to find out for yourself. It looks to us that the Buddha didn't go in for all this wishy-washy hypothetical stuff, hence his statement that we should only believe what he said when we truly believe it for ourselves. In essence, practical teachings to help you find your way along the path, like a Sat Nav for enlightenment.

Blind faith, and just believing come what may, don't seem to have a place in the teachings of the Buddha. Which leads us nicely on to Dogma. We don't actually need to say too much about this, as The Bookshelf's explanation says it all really: 'A principle or set of principles laid down by authority as incontrovertibly true,' the opposite of Dharma, or so it seems to us humble spaniels. Half-Sister sums it up nicely by referring to Mum's statement this morning, telling us that it's too wet and muddy to play in the garden. That's Dogma. We will be the judges of that one based on just how wet and muddy we actually get. Now, that's Dharma - the ultimate truth. Turns out we were right, but neglected to factor in the Ultimate Bath.

There is a strong possibility that we may be on the right track here. A kind man called Thanissaro Bhikku has written that Dharma refers to the path of practice the Buddha taught his followers. He also said that Dharma has three levels of meaning: the words of the Buddha, the practice of his teaching, and the attainment of enlightenment. That will do for us. Half-Sister is currently pondering the fact that she also has followers, albeit feline ones, and is concerned about the potential impact of a street full of enlightened cats. That's a scary thought. The Bookshelf has been studying the books collected from the monastery by Dad, and tells us the moggy meditation group could set up their own *Sangha*. He goes on to explain that the Sangha originated when a group of disciples renounced the worldly life to wander with the Buddha and listen to his teachings. When the Buddha died, they continued to live together, wandering from place to place, living off food given by others (alms). Half-Sister is now deep in thought; she thinks the cats are half-way there already. Certainly, the wandering from place to place, hanging out together and taking food from others is all in place, although it's usually out of the dustbins. It seems like they might need strict supervision from now on. Half-Sister is on it. The thought of a group of moggies following her everywhere, hanging on her every bark, does *not* appeal. The Bookshelf attempts to pacify Half-Sister by telling her that this year in the Tibetan calendar is the year of the Earth Dog, which represents loyalty, protection and friendship.

This seems to have done the trick for now - she has regained her self-important demeanour again. He decides to leave out that according to the calendar in Tibet, it's the year 2145. This is mainly due to the confrontational mess he got into with the 'raining cats and dogs' story a while back. Seems like a wise decision to me. Half-Sister has advised us that if we wish to become a wandering disciple living off food donations, we should stick to the route followed by the post lady, as she is always good for a biscuit or two. Failing that, the red kites over the supermarket would be an option. The Bookshelf chips in and suggests we do what is called a *Renunciation Practice* - giving up something we are attached to, like food for instance. He recommends we give up food for a day. Half-Sister considers this carefully and then comes to the conclusion that the best way forward is for The Bookshelf to give up chipping in. Besides, his suggestion to give up food for a day is, in her opinion, a fast- track route to the vets. How do you explain to the vet that you are not icky-sicky, but just practising renunciation? The conversation ends with

Half-Sister suggesting that The Bookshelf could become a wandering library, travelling around Buddhist monasteries, collecting their free books and distributing them to those that need some guidance on the path to enlightenment. You can tell by the shine on his wood that he likes that idea.

After dinner, Half-Sister informs us that we are going in search of the Ultimate Truth, but before we do that, we need to know what it is. So, over to The Bookshelf. Three flicks of a page and we are about to find out, although looking at his frown he seems wary about telling us. We have witnessed that frown before. It usually means he is anticipating a Half-Sister debate - not his favourite pastime.

Here is The Bookshelf's explanation of the Ultimate Truth. Make of it, what you will. We currently have headaches from excessive pondering and have gone for a lie-down.

The Ultimate Truth in Buddhism is how things really are. They are ever-changing and dependent on circumstances. Suppose Half-Sister was sad yesterday because of sad circumstances - say her food did not arrive from the Amazon man. But she is happy today because Mum got some from the shop (happy circumstances). However, she does not think she is the sad dog of yesterday; it would be untrue to say I am a sad dog because at the moment I am a happy dog enjoying happy circumstances. She cannot be happy and sad, so is not the sad dog of yesterday. She is also not the happy dog of the present moment either. Yes, she is happy now, but tomorrow, going for the daily trip round the garden, she might not be happy or sad, but neutral, so in a neutral mood. She is simply a dog, although that is just the name the humans call her for identification purposes, really. She just is. In other words, there is happiness, sadness and neutrality, but no dog is involved. There is no I, me or mine. This is the Ultimate Truth.

After exploring the explanation of the Ultimate Truth, we have learnt the following so far. Bookshelves can get headaches. We didn't know that, and maybe he didn't either. The second thing is that we might not even be dogs. We just is, apparently. Half-Sister is considering reflecting under the bamboo, but as the bamboo may not actually *be* a bamboo, she will give that a miss for now. She also tells me that she is confused, but not a confused dog. After a short debate, we have decided to resume the search for the Ultimate Truth in the morning.

That round shiny, thing that arises in the morning, and that we refer to as the sun, heralds a new day and another opportunity to establish just what the Ultimate Truth might be. Half-Sister arises from her slumber and informs us that she has been dreaming all night about what you could *definitely* describe as an absolute truth. After searching the universe in her dream, she proclaims that there are absolutely no square circles, and absolutely no round squares. It's a start. The Bookshelf agrees with Half-Sister, but is still struggling with the fact he may not even *be* a bookshelf. He has doubts now that he even exists, and is considering the possibility that all his beloved books are a figment of his imagination. He tells us that we have opened a can of worms. Thankfully, before Half-Sister launches into the meaning of that one, breakfast is served.

Once more returning to the teachings of the Buddha, we have discovered that the Ultimate Truth can only be realised through meditation, so theorising or speculating are a waste of time. This sounds good - more concentration, less headaches. The Buddha's teachings are the Ultimate Truth of the world, the first example of a scientific approach applied to questions concerning the ultimate nature of existence. Furthermore, he did this all by himself with no help from anyone (other than perhaps a bit of ball-throwing for Right Nuisance to break up the day). He encouraged everyone to follow his teachings and find out the truth for themselves. Now there is an invitation, and a motivating reason to practise meditation every day. The Bookshelf, who has been quiet of late, suddenly tells us he has found a poem that he likes and that we should consider it carefully, for he thinks it is important in helping us to understand the truth.

> *Enlightenment is like the moon reflected on the water.*
> *The moon does not get wet, nor is the water broken.*
> *Although its light is wide and great,*
> *The moon is reflected even in a puddle an inch wide.*
> *The whole moon and the entire sky*
> *Are reflected in one dewdrop on the grass.*
>
> *Dogen*

As the light fades, Half-Sister can be seen outside in the garden staring into a puddle. She can see the moon and the stars, the sky and the *whole* universe, and perhaps more importantly she can see herself, reflected on the water. Just behind her, the bamboo sways and the Buddha sits. I could swear he has a bigger smile than usual on his face.

The next morning, Half-Sister begins to explain what she discovered whilst looking in the puddle. She informs us that the only way to describe the wonder of it all is to imagine that you can press every button on the TV remote at once and see all the channels at the same time. You will then understand that all the channels are connected and all part of the package. In our house that would be Sky. Looking in the puddle you can see the whole universe, which is connected to everything. We are all part of the big picture, vibrating through the universe like TV channels on the telly.

The Bookshelf (who is happy to go along with this theory) does, however, have one reservation. He asks very politely if this means that when Half-Sister pinches the remote, she is temporarily in charge of the whole universe. When the sudden thoughts of power subside, she explains that it is only a metaphor, and he should know better than to ask, as it was he who explained metaphors in the first place.

We eagerly ask Half-Sister to explain further her theory of the Ultimate Truth, whilst being very careful not to use any more metaphors, especially any reference to worms and cans. The bit about being part of everything and that everything is connected we understand. We have an inkling about the puddle, but only an inkling at the moment. What we are wondering is what about Wandering Mind, and what part does she play in all of this?

Half-Sister ponders for a while and then gives it her best shot. She tells us to imagine that we are back looking in the puddle. This is reality in this moment. Then along comes Wandering Mind. Perhaps she is bored. After all, to her, a puddle is just a puddle. Because she is not particularly interested, she stirs things up by taking our attention away. She might go backwards in time, remembering when the ginger one next door fell in a puddle, or she might project forwards with 'what ifs' or ideas.

Wherever she goes, she is taking us away from the Ultimate Truth of what is - what is actually happening in the moment. When the Buddha says the Ultimate Truth can only be found through meditation this is because through meditation, we learn to return Wandering Mind and again see the reality of the present moment. We still the mind and therefore settle the puddle, and the water becomes clear. We did not think for one moment that Half-Sister could explain things with so much clarity. In fact, The Bookshelf has launched into an inventory, as he cannot believe she is not reading that from one of his books. Yet everything is in its place, apart from Half-Sister that is, who has gone for a walk in the garden, leaving us with all our thoughts.

As the weeks roll by, we continue to practise our meditation - sometimes in silence, other times using Dad's recordings, and occasionally guided by Half-Sister. Day by day, the muddy puddle becomes a little bit clearer. We have even stopped drinking out of the puddles on our walks. This is a great act of renunciation, as all dogs know that puddle water tastes better than tap water. However, even though it tastes nice, drinking out of the puddle completely obviates the view, and therefore takes us away from reality. Unless we are mindfully drinking the puddle water, which would be classed as a meditation practice. The Bookshelf and I consider asking Half-Sister what happens in winter when the puddle freezes over. For instance, does it mean that time stands still, like the batteries running out on the remote? After pondering this for a while, we decide to give that one a miss. The Bookshelf thinks we are bordering on a metaphor, and we all know where that one leads.

Upon hearing about our insight concerning the Ultimate Truth, Wandering Mind has denied all knowledge of creating alternative universes. She simply says it is her job to scout about, search for useful information, ideas, opinions, memories etc. She reckons paying attention to the present moment is all well and good, but sometimes you have to go and find something just a little bit more interesting. Let's face it, how exciting is a puddle when you have the whole of creation to play with or make up? Upon hearing this, Half-Sister decides to have the final say - not unusual really. She informs us that Wandering Mind is, in her opinion, deluded. She did admit that at times, Wandering Mind had been very useful, and that her imagination had produced some wonderful ideas. She had in her time also solved problems for us; however, she is a worrier and could cause as many problems as she has solved. Half-Sister suggests that through our meditation practice we can learn to understand her and therefore see if she is being useful or not, then we can choose what to do next. In the very next moment (and right on cue), Wandering Mind arrives. She informs Half-Sister that it is past her dinner time, and that perhaps the Amazon man had fallen up the steps and hurt his knee. He may now be in hospital without having delivered the food, and because of this, she might become a skeleton dog like the one that knocks on the door at Halloween. We rest our case.

Upon reflection under the bamboo

It looks to us humble spaniels as though the Buddha's teachings are pointing to the true nature of the universe - what is known in Buddhism as the Dharma. The Dharma embraces everything, including puddles, and is the opposite of the universe created by Wandering Mind. When we learn to see things as they actually are, the Ultimate Truth reveals itself to us. It also appears to be the truth that Half-Sister seems to have a handle on all this stuff. How she has accomplished this is a mystery; according to The Bookshelf, there is no book in his collection that explains this phenomena. As for Dogma, well, that's somebody else's stuff that we are supposed to believe is gospel. We would much rather go down the Buddha's path and question everything until we truly believe it. Talking about questions, here is a classic from Wandering Mind:

'Why is it not okay for her to take our attention away from the puddle, but it is apparently fine for the robin to have a bath in the puddle of Ultimate Truth?' Answers on a postcard, as we are yet to come up with a suitable reply.

Half-Sister has a poem for wandering mind:

> If this is the path
> to enlightenment
> someone please
> show me the trail
> marked ignorant bliss!
>
> Thomas Lawrence

11

The Monastery

Thousands of candles can be lit from a single candle, and the life of the candle will not be shortened. Happiness never decreases by being shared.

The Buddha

After we have finished our breakfast the following morning, Dad sits Half-Sister down and talks to her directly.

THE HOUSE IS QUIET this morning. This is mainly due to Mum having gone to one of her quilting retreats for the weekend. They are held in the Lake District in Cumbria, which by the way is where Half-Sister and I were born. She makes lovely quilts which adorn all the beds in the house. Half-Sister even has one to sleep on at the top of the stairs, although hers has additional holes (for ventilation). It also doubles as a tug toy (hence the holes). Unlike our retreat, Mum can talk, eat all day, drink wine and spend as much time on her phone as she wants. We think that 'retreat' is possibly the wrong word. Maybe 'party' would be more appropriate. We are not saying that Mum is the noisy one in the house - more like Dad is quiet, and likes to spend time in his office. Taking advantage of the peaceful circumstances, we have just been snoozing so far today, with the occasional trip into the garden - sometimes to admire the view, other times through necessity. The Bookshelf, on the other hand, has chosen to be constructive, and is passing the time organising himself in alphabetical order. If he gets really bored, he does it in reverse order. The ginger one next door can be seen from the dining room window. He is sitting on the fence facing the woods, practising his *Counting Trees* meditation. This is something Half-Sister taught him on the last meditation group session. As the forest stretches for miles and miles, he never gets to the end. It's a practice in patience. If Wandering Mind interrupts him, the giveaway sign is his swishing tail. You get the picture. It's a peaceful, uneventful and reflective day. So far.

Today is Sunday - it's the day Dad normally picks up his meditation stool and blanket and takes himself off to the Buddhist Monastery for something called *Evening Puja*. This is after he has cleaned all the dog hairs of his blanket. Oops! We have consulted The Bookshelf to ascertain what this Puja business is all about and he says Puja is a Sanskrit word for worship. However, having listened to Dad talking about it with Mum, and taking into account the information gleaned from our study days with The Bookshelf, we beg to differ. Our spaniel intuition is telling us that it may be a way of thanking the Buddha for his teachings and wisdom, rather than a form of worship. The format of the evening seems to be a bit of meditation practice, some chanting and a talk by one of the senior monks about the Buddha's teachings. This is called a *Dharma talk*. All this activity takes place in what is referred to as the Dharma Hall. All the resident monks are in attendance, apart from maybe the ones who are out wandering for food. We like the idea of a Dharma talk; The Bookshelf does a fine job, but a Buddhist monk talking about the Buddha's teachings seems like a whole new level to us. This particular monastery practises the Theravada tradition of Buddhism; we had to practise saying that one: "Terra-VAH-dah". It means 'The Doctrine of the Elders,' and takes it's inspiration from something called the *Pali Canon*. It seems to be generally agreed that the Pali Canon contains the earliest surviving record of the Buddha's teachings. The Bookshelf has a copy collected from the monastery by Dad; this discovery has Half-Sister's tail wagging in anticipation. As The Bookshelf locates the Pali Canon, a tiny little book also appears that had been wedged behind it. It's called 'A Dhammapada for Contemplation'. Presumably it also arrived after one of Dad's trips to the monastery, but may have been lost due to its size. It's full of verses about the Buddha's teachings, and has printed inside the following: 'Whatever glimpses of truth may be gained by reading, it will encourage all travellers to continue faring on.' We think that as we are travellers on the path, this little book will come in handy, especially for contemplations under the bamboo. Today we have been contemplating under the bamboo with the Buddha verse twenty. Of course, the Buddha knows it off by heart:

> *Knowing only a little about Dhamma*
> *But wholeheartedly according with it,*
> *Transforming the passions*
> *of greed, hatred and delusion,*
> *releasing all attachments*
> *to here and hereafter,*
> *one will indeed experience for oneself*
> *the benefits of walking the Way.*
>
> Dhammapada verse 20

Today, when Dad picks up his meditation stool and blanket and places them in the car, we are confused. The reason for this state of confusion is that Dad doesn't go to the monastery when Mum's away. The general consensus is that it's too long to leave us in the house unattended. They think we might get bored and get up to no good. As if! When we also end up in the back seat of the car alongside the meditation stool and blanket, we are doubly confused. Half-Sister thinks we are going to be babysat, and her money is on Wendy who lives down by the river. That thought dissolves in an instant when we drive straight past her house and head off into the countryside. Wandering Mind is in her element; she has us going everywhere from the giant hills of Scotland to the springer spaniel rescue centre. We have to admit that from what we can see out the window, our destination is a *complete* mystery. We don't recognise any of the roads, or the passing countryside. In the end, we decide to give up the destination inquiry game and just enjoy the view, although Wandering Mind is still at it and currently has us heading for the airport for our trip to India. After about twenty-five minutes, we turn off and head up a giant hill. Maybe Wandering Mind was right? When we reach the very top of the hill, there it is in all its glory. The monastery. I have never seen Half-Sister lost for barks, but today is the day. She is totally gobsmacked! I am doubly surprised – one, because Dad has actually taken us, and two, because I haven't puked in the car.

Once we have parked the car, Dad proceeds to take us to a house situated next to the monastery. At the front door, we are greeted by a lady who tells Dad she will look after us until after Evening Puja is finished. She continues by telling him that we are lovely dogs, which makes Half-Sister thinks she must be clairvoyant. Everything seems in order; it's a nice house, warm, cosy and has a real fire. I am happy enough to settle down in front of the fire until Dad gets back. The expression on Half-Sister's face, however, tells me she has no such intentions.

Half-Sister informs me that she has a cunning plan, and for this plan to succeed, I will need to play the part of the decoy. It's a responsible job, and the success of the operation hangs on my ability to pull it off. No pressure there then. She reassures me that I don't need to worry as she will be back in plenty of time, and nobody will know she's been away. This is too big an opportunity to miss. Those are her final words as she disappears out the back door and into the dead of night. Now, at home I would simply ask The Bookshelf to explain what a decoy is, but as we are in the middle of nowhere I am going to have to improvise. When the lady returns, I flip into an undignified posture and flash her my cheesiest grin. Bingo. She simply smiles back at me and doesn't even notice that we are a Half-Sister missing.

Although its dark outside, Half-Sister has no trouble finding the Dharma Hall. The lights on the outside wall of the monastery are shining bright. She can see people filing into the hall with their meditation stools and cushions at the ready, bracing themselves against the cold wind. Dad always said it was windy at the top of the hill. He wasn't kidding - Half-Sister's ears flip inside-out. There is no need for her to worry about having the correct meditation equipment. What Half-Sister is going to sit on goes everywhere with her.

Half-Sister has to wait until everyone has entered the Dharma Hall, as dogs are not allowed. She ignores that one, as there is no sign saying that, and she is *sure* the Buddha wouldn't mind. The good news is that there is no sign of the Lhasa Apso, the so-called guardian of the monastery. Obviously slacking, or on its holidays. When it looks like Evening Puja is about to begin, Half-Sister sneaks in the front door and hides at the back of the hall. Once inside, she can hardly believe her eyes! Right at the front of the Dharma Hall, surrounded by flowers and candles, is the *biggest* statue of the Buddha she has ever seen. It is towering over the hall and its occupants, and looks as if it's staring right at Half-Sister. In fact, it is so big it could fit the Buddha under the bamboo at home in its pocket, and still have room for a few carrots for Right Nuisance. Half-Sister scans the hall and is totally in awe of the spectacle in front of her. Positioned just in front of the Buddha's statue are all the monks in their splendid orange robes; they are sitting on cushions and are holding the most impressive dignified posture. Looking at their hair, they must have all been to the groomers lately. It will be a while before they need to go back. Further back are all the participants. Some are sitting on cushions, or meditation stools, whilst others are sitting in chairs. Further back again is one springer spaniel - motionless, silent, and completely mesmerised by the occasion.

Suddenly the lights are dimmed, and Evening Puja begins with three chimes of a singing bowl. This signifies the beginning of a thirty-minute period of silent meditation. Half-Sister closes her eyes, adopts a dignified posture and finds her breath. After a short while, Wandering Mind tiptoes in. "Wow, this is a cool place," she whispers. After having a good look around, she apologises to Half-Sister for disturbing her and slinks off. Now that's a new one. One thing that Half-Sister has noticed is that meditating in the Dharma Hall is very different to meditating at home, or in the garden under the bamboo. There is an energy in the hall that Half-Sister has not experienced before. Maybe it's down to the monks and all the people in the Dharma Hall meditating together, or perhaps it's all the meditation that's been practised here over the years. She wondered if it was the giant Buddha motivating everyone simply by his presence. Whatever it is, Half-Sister's meditation is deeper, concentrated and undisturbed. Apart from near the end, when Wandering Mind gently asks, "Are ya finished yet?"

The meditation session comes to an end with the sound of three chimes of the singing bowl. Half-Sister gently opens her eyes, although she is reluctant to do so, as she could have meditated for much longer. They are now moving on to chanting. Beginner's Mind will be required here, as this is certainly a new experience for Half-Sister. Everyone in the hall seems to have acquired a book of chants to help them follow proceedings, all apart from one four-legged participant that is. As The Bookshelf would have acted as a translator at home, Half-Sister decides the best option here is to just hum along quietly. Wandering Mind returns, and volunteers to join in. She suggests they could perhaps do some harmonies. Who knows, maybe they will form a band! The chanting is very hypnotic - a meditation in itself really - and lasts for twenty minutes. The words may have been unfamiliar, but Half-Sister and Wandering Mind's duet was pretty good.

The lights are now undimmed, and everyone unwinds their dignified postures and settles in for a Dharma talk by one of the senior monks. Much to the delight of Half-Sister, tonight's talk is about enlightenment. Perfect.

She listens intently, taking in every word, and then carefully handing it over to Wandering Mind to store in her memory for contemplation at a later date. Wandering Mind is being remarkably helpful this evening and, for perhaps the first time, is concentrating on the job in hand. The bottom line is that it's very much down to regular meditation practice and diligently following the teachings of the Buddha. This way, wisdom can arise and guide us down the path of enlightenment. However, we have to be careful not to strive for enlightenment, as this will only get in the way. This is tricky stuff as usual. The evening ends with another chant, but this time it's in English. Half-Sister should really be getting back to the house, but decides to stay a little longer as the chant is called 'The Buddha's Words of Loving Kindness'.

To say this chant has an impact on Half-Sister would be an understatement. She loves all of it, but this bit brings a tear to her eye:

THE MONASTERY

Even as a mother protects with her life
Her child, her only child
So, with a boundless heart
Should one cherish all living beings;
Radiating kindness over the entire world

Just as the last words of the chant unfold back into silence, so Half-Sister disappears into the night and makes her way back to the house. Halfway back, she remembers the Lhasa Apso story. She hadn't seen one but it could have been hiding, or too busy chanting to notice her presence at the back of the Dharma Hall. As she originally thought, it may have been on holiday, or not doing its job properly. Either way it was fortunate, and made the task easier.

Eventually, she makes it back to the house, which is just as well because being upside-down in an undignified posture for so long was taking its toll. Not to mention my cheesiest grin, which was in danger of becoming permanent and making me look like a character out of Wallace and Gromit. Within a couple of minutes, Dad is knocking at the door, apparently none the wiser to Half-Sister's mission. The lady says we have been good, and to come back anytime. We may well do that. In the time it takes to wag a tail, we are back in the car and heading home again. Now, my natural curiosity and nosiness leads to an extensive enquiry on the way back home into what Half-Sister made of the whole Dharma Hall experience. However, there is no information forthcoming - just a sigh, and the closing of eyes. Even Wandering Mind is absent.

All the way home we sit in silence, accompanied only by our breath, Dad and each other. Eventually we pull onto the drive outside our house - the end of another totally pukeless journey. Although, I think, I could have landed it on Half-Sister's head and she wouldn't have been bothered.

After we have finished our breakfast the following morning, Dad sits Half-Sister down and talks to her directly. We all hold our breath. Always one to get straight to the point, he asks her if she has been a naughty girl. Half-Sister puts on her best puppy eyes, tilts her head to one side and flips to an undignified posture. It's her get- out pose. This seems to have very little effect, as Dad continues to hold Half-Sister in his gaze. It reminds us of Half-Sister's tracker-beam stare she used on the ginger one next door. Dad then proceeds to confront her with a book. It's a shiny new one, apart from the teeth marks. There then follows a reprimand for chewing books. She doesn't argue. Even though she has never chewed one of Dad's books in her life, there is no growling, no circle-spinning - just total silence. Just before he leaves the house, we hear Dad talking to Mum in the kitchen. "I have never known her do that before, not even as a puppy. The funny thing is I can't ever remember bringing a book home from the monastery about enlightenment." The book is now in the safekeeping of The Bookshelf, and is studied daily by Half-Sister. There is also a copy of the chanting book tucked away in the bookshelf. Dad missed that one. Every Monday, you can hear the Buddha's words of Loving Kindness echoing around the garden as Half-Sister delivers the moggy meditation group's weekly class. She now concludes the sessions with some chanting. They all enthusiastically join in, especially the oriental one, who for all we know might speak Pali given his eastern roots.

Now, it's not just the Buddha's words of Loving Kindness that reverberate around the garden these days; Half-Sister has also picked up the habit of chanting some very strange words since she came back from the monastery. Especially if she is sitting under the bamboo with the Buddha, or about to lead the moggy meditation class. The Bookshelf has ascertained that it's Pali, but as Half-Sister has hidden the 'Learn Yourself Pali' book, and Dad has taken the computer to work, we are at a loss as to what it all means. For what it's worth, it goes like this:

Namô Tassa Bhagavatô Arahatô Sammâ-Sambuddhassa

She doesn't just say the above once, but three times. We don't have a clue what it's all about - only Half-Sister knows the answer to that one, and she is not translating. The moggy meditation group are certainly not querying Half-Sister launching into ancient tongues. They are too preoccupied with breathing in and breathing out and looking out for their Wandering Minds. Talking of Wandering Mind, there is a rumour going around the house that she knows what *Namô Tassa Bhagavatô Arahatô Sammâ-Sambuddhassa* actually means. As she was at the monastery with Half-Sister, there may be some substance to this story. Having said that, with her imagination and mischief-making, I think we will wait for Half-Sister to eventually tell us. Even though Wandering Mind has been very cooperative since she returned from the monastery, she still remains the world's authority at bending the truth. We will just have to be patient to see what else emerges from Half-Sister's monastic experience. Who knows, on our next monastery trip I might be elevated from a decoy and actually get to attend Evening Puja! That could lead to me learning to bark for my dinner in Pali. Let's see how Dad works that one out.

Upon reflection under the bamboo

We await with eager anticipation for a return trip to the Buddhist monastery, although the last one is etched in our memory forever. Half-Sister is studying her book on enlightenment and is taking her teaching responsibilities *very* seriously. Even Wandering Mind is taking an interest. I am pleased to report that the blood has returned to its usual places after the excessive undignified posture experience, and the cheesy grin is only making an occasional appearance. The Buddha has now settled into his new home under the bamboo and remains unbothered, even by the robin that has taken to sitting on his head. Everything in the household is calm, peaceful and in order, apart from Dad that is. He is still pondering the appearance of the enlightenment book and is *convinced* he didn't bring it from the monastery. Mum keeps telling him that he must have, and that he has just forgotten. She follows that up by telling him it's his age. We think that statement falls firmly in the category of unhelpful. We are still blessed with the occasional chant in Pali from Half-Sister - as yet, we still haven't a clue what she is on about.

12

The Transforming Power of Compassion

This is my simple religion. There is no need for temples; no need for complicated philosophy. Our own brain, our own heart is our temple; the philosophy is kindness.

Dalai Lama

They are all present, eager and hanging on every Half-Sister word.

TODAY, AS THE SUN rises on a new day, Half-Sister can already be seen in the garden. It's 5.30 am - this is apparently the time the monks arise at the monastery. Due to the fact that to me it is still the middle of the night, I am viewing this occurrence through one half-closed eye. Dad, who has had to get up to let Half-Sister into the garden, has decided to go to his office for some early morning meditation practice. Or a snooze. It's hard to tell. This morning's escapades are not a one-off; this has been happening every morning at exactly the same unruly hour for the past month. In fact, it's been Half-Sister's ritual ever since we returned from the monastery. Through the dining room window, we can see the sun shining its rays through the garden fence and making pretty patterns on the grass. Every now and again it shines through the bamboo that's swaying gently in the breeze. When it does this, it illuminates the Buddha in all his glory, and Half-Sister, who is sitting right next to him. She has her eyes closed and is sitting in her best dignified posture.

After half-an-hour has passed, Half-Sister saunters towards the house, being mindful not to step on any ants that have emerged for a quick circle-dance in the early morning warmth of the sun. In true Half-Sister fashion, she flops down on the kitchen floor and waits for her breakfast. Remarkably, this is not followed by endless loud barking or spinning in circles at a rate of knots - just patience personified. Now, the first time this happened you would have been forgiven for thinking that I had joined Half-Sister in the breakfast queue. You would have been wrong. My kitchen floor flop is created by shock and disbelief. If it hadn't have been for the fact that Half-Sister eats all her breakfast as usual, Mum would have whisked her off to the vets for a check-up right there and then. When Dad comes downstairs from his meditation, Mum tells him that there doesn't appear to be anything wrong with her. However, she does seem to be different somehow, but in a good way. In fact, she looks very healthy. Every morning after breakfast, Half-Sister has taken to spending time with The Bookshelf studying the Buddha's teachings. Not only that, Wandering Mind is dictating and filing things away for further reflection. Remarkably, she seems happy to do this and has set up a whole filing system so nothing gets misplaced. The Bookshelf even throws in a metaphor now and again, but they usually go unchallenged. Occasionally he looks a little disappointed. I think he secretly liked that game.

As today is Monday, morning study is followed by the moggy meditation class. They are all present, eager and hanging on every Half-Sister word. She always starts with the chant from the monastery: *Namô Tassa Bhagavatô Arahatô Sammâ-Sambuddhassa*, repeated three times. After The Bookshelf and I interrogated Wandering Mind, she finally let slip that she thought it meant *'Homage to Him'*, *'the Blessed One'*, *'the Exalted One'*, *'the Fully Enlightened One'*. Later, when Half-Sister eventually returned the 'Teach Yourself Pali' book, we were able to verify that this was, indeed, an accurate translation. It is debatable which is actually the most astonishing occurrence - Half-Sister's Zen like behaviour, or the fact that Wandering Mind has told the truth!

While we are on the subject of astonishing occurrences, about two weeks after our monastery escapades, the moggy meditation group suddenly and unexpectedly took an interesting turn. Now, a little bit of background information might help us to understand how this startling development may have come about. The instigator in this instance was the Siamese. Now we know he is the youngest, and also fearless (or daft - take your pick). We also know that when he was a kitten he grew up in a house that had a cocker spaniel. Due to his unusual upbringing, he now sees all other spaniels as potential pals. Talk about being deluded. He usual behaviour is to waltz right up to them and sit, staring, with his bright-blue eyes. Personally it freaks me out, as he just keeps inching closer and closer. Even if you bark right in his mush he doesn't shift.

On the day in question, the oriental one decided to jump the fence and position himself right next to Half-Sister. Maybe he felt extra brave that day, or is a bit hard of hearing. Anyway, there he was, eyes closed and meditating away. Now the rest of the group's reaction to this startling event was classic. First of all, and maybe not surprisingly, nobody chose to join him. In fact, they all took a step back in awe. Let's face it, it would only have been the ginger one next door that might have been up for that. The white one is a bit reserved, and the fats ones would have needed to tunnel under the fence. In fact, their steroid-induced fatness might have required planning permission from the council before we could begin the excavations. As the local council takes an age to approve these things, the idea was rejected. So they stayed where they were, wheezing in and wheezing out, but with one eye open just in case. I pressed my nose against the window and waited, while The Bookshelf read through the first aid manual.

Now, Half-Sister, even with her eyes closed, knew he was there. She simply chose to ignore him and continue with the meditation session as usual. The Siamese appeared to totally trust Half-Sister, and never once opened his eyes. Eventually, the rest of the group, accepting that the Siamese was not going to lose a life anytime soon, closed their eyes and got back to the serious business of breathing in and breathing out. On this day of astonishing events, it would not have surprised us in the slightest if the Buddha under the bamboo had turned around to have a look at meditation history in the making. When the session was over, the Siamese simply jumped back over the fence and joined the rest of the motley meditation crew. By this time, they were rolling their tongues back in and looking at the Siamese as if he were a returning gladiator having survived the games. Half-Sister strolled into the kitchen to await dinner just like any other normal day, whilst Wandering Mind instructed everyone in the house on the many ways you can scare the living daylights out of a cat.

After a further two weeks had passed, the ginger

one next door eventually plucked up the courage to join the Siamese beside Half-Sister. Although he sat further away, it was still a major step. For the first few sessions, he meditated with one eye open. We are not sure if that means he only gets half the benefit, or that only half his body is meditating. There is nobody to ask to clarify this, so we are just left to wonder. It took another month before he was confident enough to close both eyes, and for The Bookshelf to put away the first aid manual. Throughout all this, Half-Sister just continued to teach the meditation session, making sure that those on the other side of the fence felt included, and assuring them that it was okay not to be brave (or to be fat for that matter). In terms of gathering good Karma, Half-Sister may have acquired bucket-loads over the last few weeks. She has certainly gained the trust of two members of her class. But for the sake of a planning application form and a little bit of self-esteem, it might have been a full house.

It is noticeable that Half-Sister's demonstration of compassion and kindness has had a transformational effect on the moggies in the street. Especially the Siamese and the ginger one next door - they are now best buddies and travel everywhere together. The fat ones seem to be happy with their lot, and can be seen daily, sitting outside their house bringing Beginner's Mind to their asthmatic view of the world. The white one, however, just watches from afar, as if he is the observer of all that arises. Less romantically, he may have lost something. Who knows, perhaps he is dreaming of attaining enlightenment, or wondering why he is totally white apart from that silly black bit at the end of his tail.

The thought that the street moggies are searching for enlightenment is not such a far-fetched idea as you might think. The scribe previously known as Wandering Mind has been sharing snippets of what Half-Sister has been teaching them of late. According to Wandering Mind's translation, each individual has limitless positive potential, and the power to change his or her life for the better. If they practice, they can become more fulfilled, happier and contribute more to the world. Well, they certainly look happy and fulfilled; we are still waiting for the contribution bit, but it's early days.

Half-Sister followed this up by telling them that they are ultimately responsible for determining the direction of their own lives. A change of mind or heart can lead to a change in their external circumstances and affect all those around them.

Perhaps, after listening to all that information, the white one is simply weighed down with responsibility or considering his options. If they are taking the Buddha's teachings to heart via Half-Sister's instructions, then this would account for the peaceful and contemplative atmosphere emanating around the street. As Half-Sister is practising kindness and compassion to all sentient beings, it has become my job to scat the cats. It's always good fun seeing them dart off in all directions. However, I have been instructed by Half-Sister to take note of the message in the following story:

A young woman, studying in India, undertook to develop love, kindness and goodwill through her meditation practice. Sitting in her small room, she would fill her heart with loving kindness for all beings. Yet each day, as she went to the bazaar to gather her food, she would find her loving kindness sorely tested by one shopkeeper who would subject her daily to unwelcome caresses. One day, she could stand it no more and began to chase the shopkeeper down the road with her upraised umbrella.

To her mortification, she passed her meditation teacher standing on the side of the road, observing the spectacle. Shame-faced, she went to stand before him, expecting to be rebuked for her anger. 'What you should do,' her teacher kindly advised her, 'is to fill your heart with loving kindness, and with as much mindfulness as you can muster, and hit this unruly fellow over the head with your umbrella. Sometimes that is what we need to do. It would be easy enough to hit the man over the head with the umbrella. The difficult part is to do it with all the loving kindness in our heart. That is our real practice'.

Adapted from Christina Feldman and Jack Kornfield: Stories of the Spirit, Stories of the Heart.

As the story maintains, it would be easy enough to bat the cats on the head with a paw, but much more difficult to do it with all the Loving Kindness in your heart. I will do my best to master the technique. As the theory goes, practice makes perfect. Although the cats don't seem to understand that this is all for their own good in the long term.

Morning ritual

The Bookshelf has been observing Half-Sister's compassionate antics with great interest, and has been impressed by developments in the local vicinity. He thinks she is making a contribution to making our world a better place. After hearing the story about the young woman and the umbrella, he has been inspired to research the whole compassion issue. As usual, the information about the benefits of spaniels practising compassion is sparse. Surprise, surprise. For humans, however, there have been numerous scientific studies undertaken on the subject. Now, we are not sure where The Bookshelf actually got this information from, so you might need to do your own bit of digging to back up his findings. Hopefully he is correct, because it appears that developing compassion is well worth the effort. For starters, people who practise compassion produce 100% more DHEA. What's DHEA you might ask? Well, it's a hormone that counteracts the aging process. So at this rate, there might be a puppy teaching a load of kittens in the back garden in the near future! The other benefit detected by The Bookshelf is that practising compassion reduces cortisol by 23% (cortisol being the 'stress hormone'). That's two good reasons to practise compassion. We await with interest the publication of the springer spaniel research paper, but we are not holding our breath. The Bookshelf, ever the optimist, thinks we could conduct our own research and get it published in the local vet's monthly magazine. He has even come up with a working title:

The Effects of Compassion Training on a Group of Moggies with Over-Confidence, Low Self-Esteem, and Asthma. By Bookshelf, T.

He is currently consulting Half-Sister, who seems less enthusiastic. Undeterred, the thought of having his name in print is driving him on and resulting in him asking her daily.

When you are exploring the vast array of reading material in our house, it's impossible to ignore the number of books by someone called the *Dalai Lama*, the spiritual leader of Tibet. He is our Dad's favourite, and the reason he got into meditation in the first place. Conveniently, he is also considered to be the world's authority on compassion. We have been fortunate to discover a wonderful morning ritual in one of his books, and have full approval from Half-Sister to make it our opening practice each day.

"Today I am fortunate to have woken up, I am alive, I have a precious human life, I am not going to waste it. I am going to use all my energies to develop myself, to expand my heart out to others, to achieve enlightenment for the benefit of all beings, I am going to have kind thoughts towards others, I am not going to get angry or think badly about others, I am going to benefit others as much as I can."

Dalai Lama

We have substituted the word 'human' for 'canine' to spanielise the reading. As the Dalai Lama is a man of great compassion, we are sure he will not mind. For all we know, he may have a spaniel himself - perhaps even descended from the Buddha's dog, Right Nuisance.

Several weeks later, the Dalai Lama goes up even more in our estimations (if that is even possible), when we discover he apparently has a cat. In fact, The Bookshelf reckons there is a book by that name: *The Dalai Lama's Cat*. As far as we are concerned, to give up the opportunity to have a spaniel in favour of taking care of a cat is the *ultimate* act of compassion. He is truly the world's most compassionate man, and no doubt a master of clocking it on the head with all the Loving Kindness in his heart.

Upon reflection under the bamboo

After we recover from the initial shock that the Dalai Lama owns a cat, we eventually get down to reflecting on the impact of practising compassion and kindness. It seems that the ripples of compassion are filtering down the street, which is mainly down to Half-Sister's efforts with the moggy meditation group. I am sure other creatures are benefitting too, as the cats seem more interested in chilling than hunting these days. Half-Sister continues to teach all beings on both sides of the fence.

The morning ritual has embedded itself into our day - it sets an intention, and gives us purpose. We highly recommend it, and send our special thanks to the Dalai Lama. I continue to practise gently patting the cat community on the head with all the Loving Kindness in my heart. The Siamese, however, is proving a challenge. This is mainly down to his misguided belief that he is actually a spaniel. He has taken to not only staring at me with his big blue eyes, but now head butts my nose. He could be doing it with all the Loving Kindness in his heart, or alternatively he may just want a fight. I am reluctant to find out.

The Bookshelf, who has now read every book in the house written by the Dalai Lama, has posed a question regarding what will bring about the greatest degree of happiness. He has adjusted the original by the Dalai Lama to suit a springer spaniel.

Question – Spaniel version:

I believe that the purpose of life is to be happy. From the moment of birth, every spaniel wants happiness and does not want suffering. Neither social conditioning nor education nor ideology affects this. From the very core of our being, we simply desire contentment. I don't know whether the universe, with its countless galaxies, stars and planets, has a deeper meaning or not, but at the very least, it is clear that we spaniels who live on this earth face the task of making a happy life for ourselves. Therefore, it is important to discover what will bring about the greatest degree of happiness.

Dalai Lama

Answer:

Yellow tennis balls

   Half-Sister, having listened to endless quotes from the books held by The Bookshelf, has decided to add one of hers to the list. We think the Buddha and the Dalai Lama would approve of Half-Sister's new found wisdom.

Whatever side of the fence you find yourself on, there is always room for compassion and kindness.
Half-Sister

13
The World According to Half-Sister

When there is more past than future,
We begin to look inward,
To assess and know the person hidden there.
Enlightenment comes just in the nick of time.
Now that we have found it,
What shall we do with it?

Enlightenment — Stephen E Yocum

All these mysterious occurrences only added credence to Half-Sister's notion that she is the reincarnation of the Buddha's dog, Right Nuisance.

IT HAS NOW BEEN one year since that fateful day when Half-Sister and I ventured into Dad's office to explore all things meditative. I remember it well - she was supposed to be there for moral support, but ultimately snored in an undignified posture all the way through my attempts to practise the ancient skill.

Although there was a reluctance to participate, there was always a hint of interest and curiosity from Half-Sister. I just did my best and followed the instructions.

You wouldn't have thought that the Buddha's teachings would have had such a profound effect on Half-Sister if you had witnessed the very first practice we did together. The frenzied Carrot Mediation certainly gave away no clues to the unfolding of wisdom that was to follow over the coming months. The impact of practising meditation and taking to heart the teachings of the Buddha may account for the transformational process that Half-Sister has been through. However, moving from refusing to do a Body Scan Practice because it is like a CAT scan, to teaching cats a Loving Kindness Meditation in the garden, is beyond my comprehension. If I hadn't seen it with my own eyes, I would have said it was impossible. In fact, in the last twelve months, many unlikely transformations have taken place. Including Wandering Mind moving from an annoying, deluded nuisance to being Half-Sister's personal assistant and filing clerk.

With the invaluable help of The Bookshelf, we have spanielised as much information from the Buddha's teachings as our little heads can hold. This has been followed by a concerted effort to transform the teachings into action. It soon became apparent that Half-Sister's capacity to retain information and her dedication to daily meditation practice was a thing to behold. To the astonishment of The Bookshelf and I, half the stuff she came out with he didn't have in a book. We couldn't even find it on Amazon! Therefore, it stands to reason it must have been in Half-Sister's head to start with, and was just waiting for the right circumstances to come out. All these mysterious occurrences only added credence to Half-Sister's notion that she is the reincarnation of the Buddha's dog, Right Nuisance. Let's face it, how else could the information get there other than by being passed from life-to-life, as per the reincarnation theory? One thing we do know for a fact is that we will not be testing that theory using hypnotism. The Bookshelf has hidden the book on Past Life Regression, and still gets a shudder down his shelves when he remembers the experience.

As Half-Sister appears to have made significant progress on the path to enlightenment, it would therefore seem logical that she should complete this last chapter. Although she is reluctant to step into the limelight, she has agreed to do it. I do, however, have to explain that it is not an ego thing, but simply a desire to help all those beings willing to learn and improve their lives. Therefore, I am stepping back to allow you all to read the world according to Half-Sister, or Right Nuisance. Take your pick.

Over to Half-Sister

As my desire for a low-key entrance has been shattered by my younger half-sister, I will just continue on, and deal with her later. She is a bit scatty and tennis-ball obsessed, but has lots of good points. The Bookshelf and I think she might make a writer one day when she grows up (that's if she ever grows up).

The Bookshelf has informed me that when the Buddha first became enlightened, he was reluctant to share what he had discovered for fear that people would not understand. Now, I am not saying I have become enlightened here, but I do feel I may have discovered one or two important things about life. I can understand why the Buddha would not want to share his findings and the reason behind his thinking. It is wonderful, however, that he did decide to teach others. Without that decision, millions of people would have missed out on all the potential benefits, and the world would be a poorer place for it. For me, it's more about people thinking I am bonkers than not understanding what I am on about. I am a springer spaniel after all. I have noticed over the years that if Dad mentions that he has two springer spaniels, people reply by saying, 'Oh, they are lovely dogs, but a bit crackers.' So there is much to do for me to portray a wise and calm presence.

I will start with that fateful day on holiday, when somehow the book on Karma and reincarnation flew out of the Scottish bookshelf and landed on my head. Apart from changing the shape of my bonce for a while, it also shifted my whole perception of reality. After my initial fear of coming back to the planet as a dung beetle or a cat had subsided, my thoughts then shifted to what impact being reincarnated over and over again would have on the planet, and all the beings that reside on it.

Let's face it, if we knew that the Earth was our home for infinity, we would probably take care of it a great deal better than we do now. The big question is, do we want to take the chance that reincarnation might, in fact be a reality? In any case, what are we leaving behind for all the children/puppies of the future? After some serious reflection, I decided to be kind and compassionate, and to honour all beings and their environment - something I should have done anyway. If it's good enough for the Buddha, it's surely good enough for me.

Next, there is the whole issue of the present moment, or lack of it. The general consensus is that dogs live pretty much in the moment, although that's debatable watching my younger half-sister at times. Whereas human beings seem to visit the present moment only occasionally, due to their fascination with the past and the future. However, taking into consideration my study with The Bookshelf, it would appear that neither the past or the future actually exist. The past is gone, and the future has not even arrived yet, so all that's left is the present moment. Just like the man on Dad's computer said, it is all we have to work with. If we don't pay attention to the present moment, we can find ourselves whisked away by Wandering Mind, and miss that precious little piece of our life, gone forever. Wandering Mind thinks the past and the future are one big rollercoaster to play on. In the wag of a tail we can be in Disneyland with our life going up and down, and our stomach turning inside-out.

As all our experiences are taken in through our senses, so they are stored in the mind. We therefore have to be careful with our actions - otherwise, we are just giving Wandering Mind more ammunition to play with. If we are not careful, sooner or later there will be an explosion. The biggest culprits when it comes to information overload appear to be those mobile phone thingies, and the television. I knew this before I started my meditation practice and studying the Buddha's teachings. I've been taking the remote off Mum and Dad for years, but they just think it's a game. All this technology is really helpful, but if you aren't careful, it can make us even more stressed. For example, a friend of our Dad's was getting really stressed because his springer spaniel was legging it far and wide every time they went for a walk. He would lose sight of him and get very anxious, wondering how far he had gone. Along comes technology with the apparent answer - a tracking device that fits on a dog collar and links to your mobile. Now he can see where his dog is all the time. Has this solved the issue? Far from it. Now he gets anxious because he can see his springer spaniel has legged it for absolutely miles. Remember, it's not always the event that causes us to be stressed, but rather what we are bringing to it ourselves. As the Buddha explains, the difference between pain and suffering is that pain is inevitable, but suffering is optional. In other words, barking and getting stressed whilst waiting for your dinner doesn't make it arrive any faster.

As we know, the Buddha recommended we question everything until we truly believe it for ourselves. I might be recommending meditation and checking out what the Buddha said, but you should also take his message to heart. Don't believe my word as gospel - judge it on actual experience. If nothing else, you could always buy a bamboo and reflect under it. If you decide to journey down the meditation path then make sure there is the opportunity to experience sitting, walking, lying down and moving about a bit. It's fine to finish off with an undignified posture chill-out; in fact, I highly recommend it.

After the trip to Scotland for our self-imposed silent retreat in the countryside, I began to appreciate the wonder and beauty of nature, and just what a cool place Planet Earth is. Now David Attenborough has told us this for years - if you haven't seen any of his wonderful programmes then it's worth getting your teeth into the remote to check them out. Anyway, it has become pretty obvious to me that all beings on this planet are interconnected, and therefore have a place in the grand scheme of things. It stands to reason that we should just let them get on with their job, hence the Buddha telling us not to harm any living beings. He knew the score. My young half-sister's insight under the bamboo regarding the falling leaf was spot on. In that moment she saw the interconnectedness of everything, although I am not sure my winking at her in approval was fully understood. The Bookshelf understood, and was delighted that he is part of everything and connected to his roots. He celebrated the fact by finding us a quote from a man called Alan Watts. We like him - he is not only a wise man but also makes us laugh. This is one of my young half-sister's favourites:

"I seem, like everything else, to be a centre, a sort of vortex, at which the whole energy of the universe realises itself. Each one of us, not only human beings, but every leaf, every weed, exists in the way it does, only because everything else around it does. The individual and the universe are inseparable."
Alan Watts

The week we spent in the middle of nowhere surrounded by all that greenery and stunning wildlife obviously had an effect on Mum and Dad. Not long after we returned home, they splashed out and bought a holiday home in the countryside. We go up there most weekends now. There are woods to play in, streams to jump in and walks with Dad that go on for miles and miles. An added bonus is that my young half-sister has learnt how to unpuke the journey, although she still sounds like a steam train on the back seat of the car and has acquired the nickname 'Chuffa.'

Somewhere along the line we must have accrued some good Karma, because low and behold, Wendy who lives down by the river also has a holiday home just seven miles from ours! On occasions we all get to play in the woods together - a five pack of spaniels racing down the tracks and splashing through the puddles, although we have noticed that Right Side Only is getting slower and hangs out at the back. We heard Wendy say she thinks he is on his last legs. The Bookshelf is checking this out on Amazon, as they seem to sell most things, but we are sad to think that this might be a metaphor.

Using the Buddha's theory of questioning everything led me to question my relationship with cats. It turns out dogs have always chased cats. In fact, we seem to have chased most things over the years. The general consensus is that it's a food thing, driven by the need to find prey. Perhaps we are just getting in touch with our inner-scavenger. Although that theory goes completely out the window when spaniels chase motorbikes, or kids on scooters. Dad has a friend whose spaniel chases everything that is airborne; you could forgive him for chasing birds or butterflies, but to leg it after a helicopter for three fields just gives us a bad reputation.

One day as I reflected under the bamboo, a timely insight regarding cats arose in my mind. It appears that we may have been conditioned since time began - or dogs arrived - to hunt everything that moves. This is driven by the fear that if we don't, dinner might not turn up. However, dinner is now delivered by the Amazon man/woman and so far, since puppyhood, dinner has never failed to arrive (although it is sometimes late). Putting two and two together, I have realised that we are simply conditioned to believe this fear we have about going hungry. It's a prime example of automatic pilot. I think it's a good idea to explore all the things in life that might be influenced by a mind that may have been conditioned by past events and beliefs. This is where the attitude of Beginner's Mind is so powerful. Remember Jon Kabat-Zinn's quote: *"It's not that we need to seek new landscapes but rather to have fresh eyes"*.

Through contemplating under the bamboo, I have discovered many things. However, the overriding insight is that cats are just beings on this planet, and like everyone else that calls the planet home, they just want to be happy. It seemed to me that a little bit of Loving Kindness Meditation wouldn't go amiss for my new feline pals. What I hadn't realised is that they would be hungry for more, and that a whole bunch of them would turn up every week. Still, due to the demand, it made me practise even more and swat up on the Buddha's teachings so we could have a discussion at the end of each session. As for the Siamese, it seems he may either be a reincarnated spaniel, or a conditioned kitten. He has certainly let go of any fear he may have had, and appears to have unlimited amounts of curiosity. My young half-sister has given him the Buddhist name of Right Bolshie.

Finally, and for me ultimately, we come to the trip to the monastery. What can I say? I could have applied for the Lhasa Apso's job right there and then. Actually, seeing as we never saw hide nor hair of the little blighter, there might be a vacancy. The image of the giant Buddha at the end of the Dharma Hall will stay with me forever, as will all the monks dressed in their orange robes all sat in the most perfect dignified postures. Meditation, chanting and a talk about enlightenment - what more could you ask for? It was after that visit that I decided to dedicate my spaniel life to doing my best to follow the Buddha's teachings and practise my meditation daily.

Without the inspiration of my younger half-sister, who started this journey in the first place, I would still be a food-obsessed, lazy spaniel. This voyage of discovery has taught me that life is about balance - you can meditate every day and study the Buddha's teachings, but don't forget to look after your family and have fun. In my case, this means cuddle Mum and Dad, talk to The Bookshelf and chase my young half-sister around the garden. It's also recommended that you befriend Wandering Mind; she can be remarkably useful. As for enlightenment, well, The Bookshelf told me that he had read somewhere that if you think you are enlightened then you are not. How about we just leave it there. After a unanimous vote, we decided to let the Dalai Lama have the last word.

The true meaning of life

We are visitors on this planet.
We are here for ninety or
one hundred years at the very most.
During that period, we must try to do something good,
something useful, with our lives.
If you contribute to other people's happiness, you
will find the true goal,
the true meaning of life.

H.H. The 14th Dalai Lama

P.S.

Springer spaniels do not live as long as human beings; therefore, we have to move very fast to fit everything in. However, Half-Sister says it might be that we are more in the moment and so don't need to hang around as long. Because I started this book, I have decided to have the last word after all (*runs*).

Young Half-Sister

Cast of Characters

Narrator	Indi	Black/White Springer Spaniel
Half-Sister	Ella	Liver/White Springer Spaniel
Right Nuisance	The Buddha's Dog	Unknown
The Bookshelf	Himself	Wooden
Wandering Mind	Herself	Various
Dad	Gary	Human Being
Mum	Kathleen	Human Being
The Ginger One	Pedro	Tom Cat
The Oriental One	Charlie	Siamese
The White One	Max	Tom Cat
The Fat One's	Frodo and Elron	Cats
Wendy	Herself	Human Being
Combination	Lola	Sprocker
Right Side Only	Chester	Cocker Spaniel
Skeleton Dog	Spencer	West Highland Terrier

References from The Bookshelf

Ajahn Munindo. (2006). A DHAMMAPADA for Contemplation. Aruna Publications.

Bear, M., & Connors, B. (2015). Neuroscience: Exploring the Brain. Lippineott Williams & Wilkins.

Bodhi, B. (2010). The Noble Eightfold Path: The way to the end of suffering, Kandy: Buddhist Publication Society.

Bhikkhu Bodhi. (2005). In the Buddha's Words: An Anthology of Discourses from the Pali Canon (Teachings of the Buddha). Wisdom Publications.

Dr Purushothaman. (2014). What Buddha Said: Selected Sayings & Quotes of Lord Buddha. CreateSpace Independent Publishing Platform.

Gairdames, W., & Kavunatillake, W. S. (1998). A New Course in Reading Pali: Entering the Word of the Buddha. Motilal Banarsidass.

Heads, G. (2017). Living Mindfully: Discovering Authenticity Through Mindfulness Coaching. John Wiley & Sons.

Kabat-Zinn, J. (2013). Full catastrophe living: how to cope with stress, pain and illness using mindfulness meditation, rev, edn. London: Hachette.

Kornfield, J., & Feldman, C. (1996). Soul Food: Stories to Nourish the Spirit and the Heart. Bravo Ltd.

Michie, D. (2012). The Dalai Lama's Cat. Hay House UK.

The Dalai Lama., H. C. Cutler. (1999). The Art of Happiness: A Handbook of Living. Hodder Paperbacks.

Traleg Kyabgon. (2015). Karma: What it is, What is isn't, Why it matters. Shambala.

Watts, A. W. (2008). The Spirit of Zen-A Way of Life, Work and Art in the Far East (p. 152). Pomona Press.

Williamson, Marianne. (2008). The Age of Miracles; Embracing the New Midlife. Hay House UK; UK ed.

The Enlightened Spaniel

The Cat with One Life Left

Gary Heads

Illustrations by Toby Ward

1
The Path to Enlightenment – One Year On

Time. Like a petal in the wind, Flows softly by. As old lives are taken, New ones begin. A continual chain, Which lasts throughout eternity. Every life but a minute in time, But each of equal importance.

Cindy Cheney

Once we have crossed the bridge, it's full steam ahead and up the steps of The Leafy Path.

It is exactly one year since Half-Sister made the monumental decision to dedicate her spaniel life to following the teachings of the Buddha - how time flies! Therefore, it goes without saying that we are all one year older. Apart from The Bookshelf that is. He appears to have no interest in the passing of time. He always looks the same to us. Occasionally he gathers a bit of dust, and the ornaments Mum places on his head may change now and again, but, in general, he remains the fountain of knowledge that has never let us down on the path to enlightenment. It wouldn't surprise us if he was the last man standing at the end of time (we think the Amazon man might come a close second).

Throughout the year we have diligently followed the Buddha's teachings, and continue to do our best to put them into practice. Under the bamboo in the back garden remains our chosen place for reflection. The bamboo, however, has grown, and apart from casting an even bigger shadow over the garden, it now provides complete shelter from the rain. The Buddha's statue that Dad carefully positioned at the base of the bamboo has also changed. Over the year it has acquired some splendid green moss. We think it makes the Buddha look rather distinguished, and its presence has attracted an abundance of tiny birds who delight in taking turns to sit on his head. We would hazard a guess that he is unbothered by this feathery development.

The Bookshelf, having taken it upon himself to unravel the workings of Karma and reincarnation, has yet to make any progress regarding Half-Sister's premonition that she is the reincarnation of the Buddha's dog, Right Nuisance. Half-Sister is convinced that she is, and has suggested to The Bookshelf on many occasions that there is no need for further research. That will not stop him - once on a mission, he will not rest until he has the answer. Regardless of what Half-Sister says in public, we know she dreams of one day having the official stamp of approval.

As far as the moggy meditation group is concerned, there is no doubt in their minds that Half-Sister has connections to the Buddha. They hang on her every word, and practice their meditation as if their lives depend upon it. In the past year, with Half-Sister's guidance, they have been transformed from a bunch of street-fighting assassins into a fully-fledged Buddhist sangha. Although every cat within the group is of equal standing, The Ginger One Next Door definitely has his sights firmly set on attaining the position of Half-Sister's assistant. I am not sure he is up to holding down such a responsible position. Just the other day she suggested that, with more effort, he could take his meditation practice to a higher level; since then, he has taken to meditating on car bonnets. He is perhaps not the sharpest pencil in the box, and is potentially one sandwich short of a picnic.

It was on last year's holiday in Scotland (a silent retreat) that revelations began to arise in the mind of Half-Sister. She was never quite the same after that. The experience of spending so much time in nature has worked its magic, and we now have our very own holiday home in the heart of Northumberland. Well, Mum and Dad bought it, but as everyone knows, everything belongs to springer spaniels. Now we can have a silent retreat whenever the mood take us, and embark on long walks in the countryside. Good Karma all round. At our new abode, we even have a ruined castle just around the corner! It has trees growing out of the windows and the roof, and it casts a spooky shadow in the moonlight on our late night saunter.

We do, however, feel a little guilty leaving The Bookshelf behind, as we are sure he would love it here. He assures us that he is fine, and passes the hours reading about Benjamin Franklin, who started the Library Company in 1731. Half-Sister hopes he's not lonely.

Last year's surprise visit to the Buddhist monastery has yet to be repeated. On that day, Half-Sister's decision to creep into the Dhamma Hall and join in with the Evening Puja turned out to be the defining moment in her decision to follow the Buddha's teachings. We are eager to revisit this wonderful place and have the opportunity to meditate and chant with the resident monks and participants. Wandering Mind still talks enthusiastically about the whole experience, especially the part where she harmonised with Half-Sister in the chanting, and took notes. I missed out that day as I was busy being a decoy. It was my distraction technique that enabled Half-Sister to sneak out un-noticed. The nice lady who looked after us never suspected a thing (thanks to my fine decoyness). Next time, things will be different. We have no idea when Dad will decide to take us to the monastery again, but we know he will one day. Until that fateful day arrives, we are simply biding our time. Apart from the occasional anticipation induced spin.

Once again, I have been entrusted with narrating the ongoing story. I must have done a half-decent job on the last one. Either that, or nobody else wants the job. So, here we go....

Available now